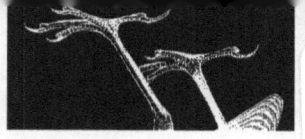

Final State

www.finalstatepress.com

The Double Ǝ

a novel

Matt Briggs

for Lisa Purdy

The Double E

Contents

The Woodchucks Will Triumph

Marshall

M arshall pockets the key off his stepfather's ring while his stepfather showers. Mist floats through the cracked door. The drops swirl and stick to the hardwood floorboards. His stepfather's pants hang from the hanger where Roger Carnation hooked them when he came home. His pressed white shirt drapes unbuttoned on the counter. Marshall leans through the humid shower room air and squirms his hand, his thumb folded to his palm, his fingers collapsed into a single triangular point, until the sensitive pad of his middle digit brushes the cool, oblong key metal. He rocks the edge, slips his index into the key ring and draws the mass of brass and steel and rust from the fabric, lint and receipts so crumpled from travel that they are as soft as tissue. He passes through the door and into the hallway. Holding all but the one key he wants, a tiny and thin skeleton key, he wiggles it loose from the ring and then he drops the heavy clump back into the pocket hole with a metallic clink.

Through school, Marshall presses the key in his front pocket against his thigh. Rather than eating lunch with his friends, Burl and Tom, Marshall takes his brown-paper-bag lunch and walks to McLendon's Hardware store. The place is full of carpenters and plumbers at the lunch hour, buying plywood and copper pipe. Lumber trucks with thin racks heaped with moldings, plumber vans, trucks with the A-frames to hold plate glass, stuff the lot. "Good morning, what can I do for you, son?" the man at the key counter asks him. The machine grinds into the copper alloy blank with a stop sign handle. The man hands Marshall both keys back. The key feels warm and has tiny particles of metallic dust clinging to the new teeth. Marshall eats his lunch in the park overlooking the Cedar River. Black water hides the salmon returning to the hatchery. When he returns home, Marshall enters the garage and unlocks the padlock and climbs into Roger Carnation's plywood camper. It sits removed from the bed of the Ford truck in the garage. It's a hut. It sits in the middle of the garage in plain view, but Marshall has never been inside before. A small staircase ascends from the cement floor to a tiny doorway locked with a brass padlock. The floor is coated with a layer of engine oil furry with dust and stray lint from the clothes dryer. He insert a key and steps through a doorway so tiny he has to turn sideways to edge into the hut. He can barely see in the plywood camper. Drapes cover the small portholes. Marshall finds the switch and presses the brittle plastic lever until it snaps forward. Nothing seems to happen at first. An old moving lantern flickers on. A tall cone holds an image of Mount Rainier looking down on the Snoqualmie Falls. Gigantic Douglas fir trees grow above the cliffs. The clouds move and billow as the cylinder rotates in the lamp heat. The animated cascade flows over a cliff lip. Clouds of spray billow across the river pool. In the dark forest, on the backside of the cone, a sixteen-point buck jumps out of the blue. Its yellowish hide and the curls of fur wave in an animated froth. Dangling high over the glaciers of Mount Rainier, the words, "Mount Rainier Beer," remain steady as the entire panorama turns around. The rest of the room rests in shadows that grow darker away from the lamp. The lamp sits on a side table constructed of deer bones. Bolted to the wall behind the truck cab, a gun rack holds a Winchester .45, a thin Smith & Wesson .22, a Sears and Roebuck shot gun. A half-empty bottle of Jack Daniel's sits on the floor by the chair next to an ashtray with a cigar stub and a single water glass. The camper smells like smoke and dust and gun oil, a smell that Marshall sometimes smells on Roger Carnation and every so often on his sister Martha, a smell he can't really place but that now he realizes comes from this shadowy recess. He opens the chest against the other wall and finds a backpack, pack tightener, rubber hip waders, folded fishing poles, and magazines—*Playboy* and *Modern Photography*—and more bottles of whiskey. He is afraid of the time he has left. Without thinking, he takes a copy of *Playboy*, something; he isn't sure why he takes something but he wants to know he's finally made it into Roger Carnation's space. Marshall locks the door. Passing his parents' bedroom he puts the key in a pair of Roger Carnation's dirty slacks.

He hides the magazine in an old envelope and tucks it into the space under the bottom draw of his dresser.

Marshall snaps the trombone onto the bicycle rack with the pack tightener and leaves for band.

The tires of his stepfather's blue Dodge Dart hum on the asphalt and then crackle on the gravel. Marshall doesn't wave, but keeps the pressure on the handles and pumps the pedals. The wheels of his bike pass from the vibrating crunch of gravel to the smooth, whir of the solid asphalt.

Marshall takes the shortcut through the park, down the paved road. The roots of the cottonwoods have cracked the paving, leaving hunks of loose tar and crumbling and gravelly asphalt stones on the shoulder, and the smell of muck hanging over the road. Thin green shoots with dime-sized leaves poke through the holes. A long highway railing blocks the road. A posted sign reads, Foot Traffic Only. Marshall vaults off his bicycle, and the weight of the trombone that he'd been countering, although he hadn't realized he'd been counteracting, swings the Schwinn around, twisting the handles out of his damp palms and whacking the handlebar end against the ground. The nut holding the bars to the frame loosens and the handles bend sideways. The trombone case bounces on the pavement.

Picking the bike up and then scooting it around the roadblock, Marshall counters the weight of the trombone and then peddles across the park. The handle jiggles loosely against the crossbars. A stream gurgles down a deep gully. Rotting red, five-pointed leaves and mulching, webbed silver oval leaves flow over the park, killing the already whitish and pale strands of overgrown grass. The dirt smells sweet, not like sugar but more like honey. The stream flows between the clay banks of the gully, a deep brown and green riling movement of water. Marshall rides the Schwinn over the stream. A whiff comes from the water; the fishy odor of the spawning salmon. Carcasses float in the river. They've already laid their eggs in the gravel upstream in the forest and float back downstream. On the other side of the park, Marshall rides past the houses lined along the county road and then finally past the gate under the marquee that reads *Homecoming Week October 15-22, The Woodchucks Will Triumph.* Marshall reads it to remind himself he doesn't care.

After school on a Friday the parking lot doesn't

have any cars except for the ones in the band parking lot behind the shop class fume-hood and delivery door. Tasty Hank, the janitor, walks on the sidewalk skirting the empty parking lot. He is Tasty Hank instead of just Hank because Burl heard Tasty Hank say to another janitor during the Pep Rally for Homecoming, "She's a tasty little thing." He said this about the Homecoming Queen. She stood at the top of the stage with her court, the Homecoming Queen runners-up arranged below her. She held a bouquet of white roses already beginning to go black at the edge of the petals. With her other arm she waved, a practiced, precise tilt to her hand.

Tasty Hank wears a sawdust-covered plaid work shirt. Even though he's a normal-height , Tasty has a very long upper torso and short, thick legs. He has long, muscular arms. The tendons stand in relief on his neck and his arms. The tendons coil as Tasty Hank carries the long limb-cutting tool. The crescent of the cutting blade clacks on the cement sidewalk. He grunts as Marshall bikes past him, and then Tasty turns to walk up the hill through the fir trees toward the high school's upper parking lot. A stand of tall cedar trees lost limbs and tops during Thursday night's windstorm. The branches are in the baseball field. The wind blew leaves and stray bags against the walls of the school.

When Marshall stops the Schwinn, the heavy trombone pulls the bike over again. The handles twist free of his hands and the frame of the bicycle scythes his legs. He keeps his balance and then unfastens the case from the bike. He locks up his Schwinn and runs with the trombone bumping against his legs up the back steps to the band room door.

Burl and Tom stand in the shadows under the fire exit steps to the auditorium. The fire exit doors don't have any handles. They wear their Marching Band Uniforms, blue pants with red leg stripes and brass-buttoned blue coats with tangled, dingy epaulets. Their conical blue marching hats sit on the wet pavement. "Marshall, you're late."

Everyone knows that the conical hats look like dunce's caps or old-fashioned clowns and so no one likes to wear them.

"I'm here, aren't I?"

"So what's the story?" Burl takes a drag on his cigarette. He holds the cigarette with his thumb and forefinger. He's just started using this smoking technique, and says he is going to France in the summer and he says, "In the autumn, I'm going to depart on the Trans-Siberian Railroad and defect to the Soviets." Burl pulls his cigarette away from his mouth as if he is drawing a string out of his esophagus, and asks, "You going with us this summer?"

Marshall looks at Tom. Tom hasn't stopped looking at him. There is a pause as the smoke swirls around in the windy eddy on the fire escape steps, where the three friends look one another over. Burl holds himself up. Tom raises his eyebrows.

"Sure. I'll go with you," Marshall says.

"You aren't going." Burl drops the half-smoked cigarette on the ground, and then he stomps it out with a twist of his boot. Tom follows behind him and then Marshall comes along.

"I can't afford to go to Russia to defect," Marshall says. "I have to get a job."

"It isn't about money," Burl says. "It's about doing something meaningful with our lives. What's some stupid summer job mean to your life? You don't need money in Russia. That's the whole point."

The band door opens and lets out a burst of the warming-up band room noise. Trumpets climb their scales. *Ah beeflat see dee eeh eph gee.* Marshall feels the deep discordant vibration of the tuba *ompa umbo umpa umbo* in his chest cavity. The majorette plays her piccolo. It is a shrill tweet, a shrill screech. Betsy stands over the sink sliding out curls of brass French horn tubing and splattering spit into the drain.

Marshall cuts down the hallway and into the locker room. He removes his uniform from his locker. It is recently dry-cleaned and smelling like starch and still in tissue paper and plastic. He strips the paper off the uniform. The thin plastic feels like a fist of oil, so thin it seems to melt on his skin. He straps the plastic loop of the conical hat to his head. The trousers have shrunk in the dry cleaners. Or his legs have swollen. They are too tight around his thighs and too short at his ankles.

He leans down to stretch his pants legs down. He grunts and pulls. It doesn't make any difference.

Marshall has become preoccupied with his looks. He has been growing out his hair and letting his sideburns get shaggy. When he used to think about what he looked like, which admittedly wasn't often, Marshall generally considered how best he could be unobtrusive. He preferred to look at other people and think about what they were doing. He didn't want anyone to notice him. While hiding unobserved in his usual position, he once heard Betsy say she wanted to date someone who looked like Samuel Taylor Coleridge. She said all three names, separating even the syllables. Marshall heard all kinds of things from his unobtrusive point of observation, and probably wouldn't even remember this particular statement except that after school that day on the way to his Schwinn he passed Betsy in the hallway. She was walking and looked right at him and didn't say anything to him but kept walking toward the buses. She had looked at him but looked at him like she was looking at the wall, as a point of reference so that she wouldn't bump into the wall or bump into him. He thought if only she knew about him, if only she knew that he was like Samuel Taylor Coleridge. Or perhaps, he realized that in cultivating an unobtrusive position of observation, he had become invisible. So he vowed to grow his hair long and practiced a kind of manic stare in the mirror. "What's wrong with you?" his sister Mary had asked him. "Are you all right?" He isn't all right.

Mr. Meredith, the band teacher, walks through the locker room. "Come on, Marshall, everyone is getting on the bus." He wears a black tuxedo. The cuffs and the elbows are threadbare. He wears a red bow tie. Mr. Meredith has pale blond hair and always looks like he has been holding his breath. His face is red and his flesh is so transparent that Marshall sees through the top layer of skin to the map of finely branching veins. Mr. Meredith grows a mustache. It doesn't really look like a mustache, but instead the clear and thick hair looks like bristles of a brass horn cleaner attached to his purple lip.

Marshall follows Mr. Meredith. He has his trombone. Everyone else has cleared out of the band room and the lights are low. Everyone is in the bus already. Marshall bumps and bangs his trombone case down the aisle. Mr. Meredith sits behind the bus driver. Burl and Tom sit in the back and he can hear them saying that they want Americans over there so they can show the U.S. the superiority of the Soviet system. People are defecting because they are sick of TV commercials.

Even though they've kept a seat for him in the middle of the wide backseat, Marshall sits in the first empty seat behind Betsy. He is sick of talking about Russia. He wants to say something to her. He looks at her hair and her French horn case sitting like a passenger on the aisle next to her. He puts his trombone on his seat, behind her French horn. The bus lurches forward. The lights dim.

Betsy reads a book and she leans close to the window and holds the V of the open book to the window to see better in the fading daylight. Marshall leans forward to see what she is reading but his only good view is from the reflection of the book in the window and he can't read very well in reverse. Even though the sun has set and the streets are dark except for the orange light under the streetlights, the sky is still a glowing raspberry blue. Faint pink clouds scuff the horizon and through the last of the daylight Marshall can faintly see the beginnings of the stars.

Everyone pours out of the bus. A wind comes across Lake Washington, up the Cedar River, and smells like milfoil and rotting salmon. The band trails through the gate and across the Astroturf field. On the fifty-yard line, everything is just the field. The sky can't be seen past the banks of bright lights too bright to look directly at and too bright to see past. Burl shuffles right up behind Marshall, and Marshall can hear him coming up because he is still talking to Tom. They are talking about going to school as far away from Seattle as they can get. Burl wants to study Spanish in Miami, join the CIA, and become a double agent for the Soviets—this is his other plan, which is to stay in the US and work for the enemy.

Although he hears Burl approach and Marshall has shifted his weight forward, waiting for the kick, it still catches him by surprise. Marshall tumbles forward and almost knocks Betsy down. Marshall feels his back leg turn sideways. The Astroturf holds a lot of water. His thigh and knee turns from blue to dark blue to almost black. Marshall doesn't say anything, but jumps back up to his feet without losing his grip on the trombone handle. He keeps walking with the band across the field. "Watch your step," Burl says.

They are in the bleachers, Burl and Tom play trumpet

and sit down, toward the front, six and seventh chair among twelve instruments. Marshall, the only trombone player, plays first chair.

He sits down right behind Betsy. Everyone puts together their instruments, the sound of clacking tin and brass and then the occasional toot and a scale, discordant and off-key in the stadium's cold air. The air feels icy on the black, damp fabric on Marshall's knee. He tries to dry it with his polishing cloth, but it leaves lint and stray hair on his knee without getting his knee dry. Betsy shoves the bell of her horn between her legs and then takes out her book. In the floodlights, Marshall can read it. *The Rainbow*. Everyman Library Edition. It's worn along the back spine, missing the jacket.

"What are you reading?" he asks her.

She holds the book up.

"Have you read it?

"I'm reading it now."

"Oh. Right."

She turns back to her book.

"Sometimes I reread books."

"Yeah?"

"That's why I asked. I'm not a complete idiot or anything."

She turns and looks at the rest of the row, people with their instruments in their laps or playing parts of songs. *Sweet Georgia Brown. Lay Down Sweet Chariot For Momma is Going to Bring Me Home.* Betsy has milky skin, vanilla malt granules of crushed ice skin. She has skin Marshall could drink and get a milk mustache. A tarnished tin clasp holds her unwashed hair back. She smells faintly of hair oil and dandruff, a scalp odor, hidden under rose water. Marshall likes the talcum powder of dandruff. He doesn't like the rose water, which is a soap smell. Her fingernails have paint particles or crayon wax, bright apple green and raspberry blue and lemon yellow, under the nails. Reddish, irritated skin and scabs cover her hands. Her arms are washerwoman arms. She smiles at him, exposing crooked teeth.

"Your name is Marshall, right?"

"I've read that book. Lawrence is okay. *Sons and Lovers. Women in Love. Lady Chatterley.*"

"*Lady Chatterley's Lover.* That's a dirty book."

"Have you read it?" he asks.

She rolls her eyes.

Mr. Meredith taps his music stand with his baton. The stadium has started to fill. The football teams spread out on the field in their formations jumping up, arms and legs spread, and then land on the balls of their feet, legs together. They are jumping jacks. One, the cadence calls out, four, six, ten. The band plays *Stars and Stripes Forever, The New World Symphony, When the Saints Come Marching In.* The brassy clank and bellow of music surrounds Marshall. He never practices, but carries the trombone case, full of the trombone, the trombone full of spit, from band to the house, leaves it in his bedroom, and then carries the trombone case, full of the trombone, the trombone full of spit, back to the band room. First chair is also last chair. While he reads the music, which he can read and so he can muddle through most tunes, Mr. Meredith attends to the fractured trumpet section. They play the melodies for the most part. If they aren't playing in time even someone who doesn't know the song might be able to tell something is wrong. Sometimes the tuba player, who tends to lose count, loses count. How hard is it to count one, two, three, four? The tuba player loses count. Mr. Meredith points to him and makes a cutting motion to his own neck and restarts him again at the beginning of a measure.

Betsy was in Marshall's first gym class. She wore purple

shorts and he wasn't very nice to her because she was so ugly in her purple shorts with her white legs. She had to spot him while he climbed the rope and then he spotted her while she climbed the rope. He stood back five steps from the rope and made sure that if she fell, she wouldn't land on him. She didn't fall, but she could tell by his not looking at her that he hadn't been spotting her. She didn't understand. Maybe this was how Marshall had first started thinking about Betsy, his guilt over being repulsed by her, because later on that first day of seventh grade, he sat behind her in band and he wanted to say something to her, some joke about her playing the French horn and him playing the trombone—there was something about the curls of brass tubing—but an opportunity never presented itself as it might between him and the trumpet players when they worked out a part where it was important to hear the slide of the trombone. After that first day they had settled into a sort of general avoidance of each other.

While Marshall muddles through the score, he sees Roger Carnation walking down the aisle in front of the band, ducking under Mr. Meredith's waving and conducting arms, the whole time keeping his eyes fixed to the front of the stadium where the cheerleaders, spread equidistant from each other, stand on bright red drums in their short blue skirts. Their livid legs shine almost purple in the cold air. They keep warm by rolling their pompoms and singing over the discordant howl of the band, "We've got Spirit. Yes We Do. W - O - O - D. Yes Wood. C - H - U - C - K - S. Yes WoodChucks." Mary and Marshall's mother walk behind Roger Carnation. Marshall's mother carries a brown grocery bag. She says something to Roger, but he doesn't stop walking ahead. Mary looks at the band and then waves at Marshall. He lifts his pointer finger as he slides the trombone.

Roger Carnation, when he first saw Marshall carrying

his horn to school one morning, asked him what was in the case.

"Trombone."

"Let's hear it."

"I'm going to be late for school."

"Let's hear it."

He took it out and then played some of a song he was surprised he could remember. It wasn't much. Most of his songs were just *pom pom pom* and so on. He performed a slide at the end, *pom pom pom pom po-ah-ohm*.

Roger clapped. "Yep. A trombone is only for a burlesque girl on a Parisian stage that'll suck your cock for five francs," he said.

Halfway through the second quarter they shuffle down into the locker room to get ready for the half-time show. They stand in their positions. Marshall stands directly behind the tuba player. They stumble onto the track, past the chain link fence, and out onto the plush green field. He finds his mark on the 35th yard line. The rain falls from the darkness above the floodlights in long rainbow-filled arcs. Marshall can barely hear the other instruments as they sound. The entire song vibrates from a great tinny distance. He blows and the trombone rumbles and drowns out the other instruments on the Astroturf. He counts out his time. He takes his calibrated steps. He plays his notes into the echo between him and the other players. Weekday drills have left the movements as routine as brushing his teeth. Out on the field it doesn't seem like there are any people in the stadium. He can barely see past the glare of the lights and the sheets of falling rain. Betsy passes him, in line with the flank of flutes and clarinets. She is supposed to have a special marching horn, but a valve broke during the weekday practice. Now she holds her own French horn, leaning into it as she marches. Marshall points the bell of his trombone toward the hazy sky. Raindrops fall from the clouds through the floodlights and into his horn. He turns half right. He takes three steps forward. Double-checks his position with the tuba. He turns a full right. He steps into the line and follows the leader. He lays the same three notes, G B D and slides back to G B D and slides back.

Finally, the band shuffles from the field and stands in the hallway leading into the locker room. The damp, warm air of the showers and the odor of antiperspirant oozes along the cinder-brick walls. They pass around towels to dry the brass bells of their instruments. The rim of the horn chills his fingers.

As he puts his horn back into its case, Betsy asks Marshall if he would like a smoke.

He doesn't say, "I don't smoke." They go to the front of the stadium and stand under the line of trees planted to protect the field from the wind. It's dark there. They can see the river and then the stadium and the field. The half-time show really begins then. The floats with the returning Homecoming Queen follow the current Homecoming Queen and her court. Most of the girls still wear their cheerleading skirts and WoodChuck sweaters. The boys wear football shoulder pads and numbers. Laura O'Brien, though, wears a yellow dress. She holds the stem of a white umbrella in her right hand and waves with her left hand, sheathed in a yellow glove.

Betsy and Marshall huddle under the poplar trees. Samaras, blown in from the maple trees, arc in wide spirals, bouncing into their faces with sharp bites. A shaggy layer of moss grows on the pavement. Roots have cracked the surface. Betsy rustles the cellophane-wrapped cigarettes. She offers Marshall one. He takes it. He knows how to pretend to smoke without coughing, but she watches him.

"You aren't dragging on the cigarette."

"I don't smoke much," Marshall says.

"Hasn't anyone taught you?"

"How do you teach someone? This is smoking. This is all there is to it. You light this end. You suck on this end."

"It's not just about burning the cigarette. The smoke is the good stuff. It needs to get into your lungs where the nicotine will rush to your head."

She takes his cigarette.

"Watch, you suck it in and then you pull it into your lungs like you were coming up for air at the pool." She gulps and then she exhales.

He does that and there is a burning deep ache in his throat and then he feels a flash and warmth. The river rolls and they can hear the voices in the distance for Homecoming. They don't say anything. She stands in front of him with both legs planted on the ground, a bulk of thighs and butt and hips and chest. She sees him looking at her and she says, "Are you enjoying your view?"

"I am not." He doesn't know what to say. He repeats, "I am not—looking at anything. If I were, I'm sure I would be enjoying the view. But I'm not looking at the view because that would be rude."

She steps forward so her entire body presses up against his and he presses up against her and he doesn't back away although he wants and doesn't want to. She is about to push him over. Marshall stands against her and she takes another drag. She says, "Come on," and he follows her back to the gate and back into the bleachers. An old couple stands at the base of the stand. "Betsy," they say, "why don't you come up and sit with us?" She says, "All right," and leaves Marshall among the bunched coats, the stray conical marching hats, and the empty instrument cases. He looks after her and he doesn't want to go sit with Mary and Aileen and Roger Carnation. He sits down and looks at the people walking back and forth.

Tasty Hank stands in front of the bleachers. When he sees Marshall sitting alone with the instruments, he nods and takes several giant steps with his short legs. When he sits down next to Marshall, he seems taller than Marshall. He has odor; a cloud of smell: sawdust, gasoline, engine oil, and liquor.

"You seen the Homecoming Queen?"

"Yeah."

"I'd like to get me some of that."

"I'm sure you would."

"But guys like us have to make do with what guys like us can get. Am I right?"

Aileen

Two o'clock. A slice of toast from the new loaf of bread before the noisy grade school kids hoop and holler and fill the street. The girls and Marshall will want to open the icebox. What has Aileen done today? Justification. A prepared statement ready to disarm guilt before Roger's evening interrogation. He'll sneak in at dusk smelling like work, cigarette smoke in his graying sideburns, graphite on his fingertips, splotches of rain damp on his overcoat. Hon. Kiss on her cheek and she will feel the pebbles of his teeth. What did you get done today? Roger will smile. The serrated and wrinkled skin around his eyes will crease deeper. He'll show his canines and sharp-edged front teeth, faintly cracked, yellow at their edges. He doesn't show his teeth when he smiles unless he's planning on chewing through something, like gnawing the corn on the cob or mauling barbecue soused ribs. What has she done today? This and that. That and this. Doesn't the house look clean? They will sniff the remnants of the Lysol cloud. As it burns the tiny blonde hairs from their nostrils, Roger will grunt and go to the bedroom to change.

Aileen considers saying to those shattered teeth, Nothing, Roger. Should she? Justification and a clean house aren't too expensive. Before Aileen dusts the house, wipes the fixtures, vacuums, though, she sits on the couch and balances the lunch plate on her apron and eats the liver and onions while she watches TV. She eats the leftovers from last night, liver and onions fried up again in a pan with butter. The girls can't do this. Grease stains on the cushions. Say it appeared there. A weather report on the TV. The anchor looks so handsome in his double-breasted suit standing in front of the map of the cold front. The dark square wedges line up over the squiggly lines. They are variations in temperature. The weatherman holds his pointer stick, a military commander explaining the maneuvering of the troops. 55 degrees and partial sun breaks.

The football game will be nice tonight. Roger lets Aileen sing along and shout at the referees. Doesn't notice, maybe. Doesn't complain, regardless. Low of 45 degrees. 360 degrees in a circle. Hot enough to cook a steak. Probably not the same system degrees temperature as degrees in a circle. Wears her twin set. The future already known. Low of 45 degrees means chilly at the stadium. She swallows the slips of onions. Chews on the spongy refried liver.

The kitchen smells oily like onions like a kitchen like a place where cooks cook food and eaters eat food until she mops the floor, rinses down the counters, dusts with an ammonia-soaked rag and then lifts the cool, heavy green can of Lysol. She depresses the yellow nozzle. A cloud of toxically clean scent floats over the linoleum, gassing the germs. She watches each drip drift through the air. Drops crash in a tiny puddle landing and fuzz at the edges. Peroxide fuzzes an infection. Aileen walks through her chores, she thinks of them as her debts to Roger, not able to prevent his occasional inspection of the house, his military manner picked up like the clap. Shouldn't think that, *that's the problem with her*. His military manner, stiff back, contracted in a submarine in the Pacific but social diseases can be cured by modern science. A military manner requires an ice pick carefully inserted through the right eye socket. A house is a machine. That's Roger. She imagines Roger in reverse circumstances, scrubbing gunmetal until it gleams for some distant admiral who enters the submarine in his white uniform and white gloves. Her first husband, Orson, didn't care about the clean floors. It was impossible to keep a tarpaper shack clean, regardless, and when the Honorable Fallon sent him to jail and she worked at PEMCO Insurance earning not enough time and not enough money to keep the house clean. Martha's feet grew or her shoes grew smaller. Blisters formed on Martha's toes. They curved into each other and the doctor told Aileen that Martha needed new shoes or her feet would be deformed. Same principle as Chinese foot binding.

Aileen rolls the vacuum cleaner canister into the middle of the carpet. Unrolls the cord. Heavy and thick, she drops the wire on the carpet. She walks away from the Hoover and stands at one end of the room. Takes the dusting rag from the closet and walks back across the room and dusts. She takes down the porcelain figures on the shelf over the front window one at a time and sets them on the couch. She flicks the rag over the cobwebs on the shelf. She sets the horses and the cattle back. Garbage, really, little lambies Martha brought her, the nose a black smudge. Eye slots curl like turned over parentheses. Martha has to buy her mother a birthday present, so she buys her anything. *Oh Ah. How lovely*, Aileen says when she opens the tight little department store packages knowing it will be another figurine she won't know what to do with aside from carefully removing it while she dusts the living room. *You'll have a whole farm in no time*, Martha says. Aileen prays for an earthquake like the one in 1957 that rattled the whole house and broke some plates. A bridge-collapsing earthquake to shatter the lambies and the farmer and his wife, the yellow, rearing mustang, the sow with the little daubs of fired porcelain that didn't look like anything except shiny mouse droppings but were supposed to be piglets. Martha doesn't know about farm life, really. She never hauled slop out for the pigs, their mouths stinking shit pits lined with rotting green teeth and black gums. Pigs don't say *oink oink* like children make them say. *Horrnk. Horrnk*, more like it. *Cock-a-doodle-do*, the American rooster says. *Coo-ca-re-coo*, the German rooster says. But animals don't speak language.

The rubber Hoover plug is warm and ribbed like a long pig's tail.

The noise of the vacuum cleaner is the worst noise in the world, like the electric saw blade her father ran in his barn. The canister sings *WHOOO WHOOO WHEEE*. She bangs the tube against the couch legs and the coffee table legs and the moldings down the hallway. Aluminum tube vibrates in the soft skin between her finger and thumb. What's it called? The palm fold. Electricity bothers her, plugs, and the blue spattering arc when she unplugs the coffee percolator. Just before she left home, the county strung wire out to the family place. The Sunset Highway place where Orson moved her when she was pregnant with Mary had a hand-pump and outhouse and no wires. Not even a phone. Roger moved her into this house with carpets and flush toilets and a phone. She can call anyone if she had anyone to talk to. She can call the police, but they won't help. Roger says electricity is safer than the fireplace. Aileen grew up in front of a cast iron stove. She keeps thin twigs piled by the stove to modulate the heat to make pies the way her grandmother made pies, hunched in front of the oven with all of the doors and windows open. Use the range, Roger says. Save yourself some trouble. We're in the twentieth century, now.

When she puts the vacuum cleaner back, she hears the insides of the house ticking and then a softer sound like the vacuum. *whoo whoo whee.* The furnace turns on, filling the house with dust and the faint odor of natural gas. Can't be good for you. Blinding headaches. Onset indicated by squiggling transparent caterpillars.

She pours a cup of coffee and drinks it and sits at the table and looks at the row of scraggly poplar trees. Worn whisk brooms against the billowy clouds. She opens the cupboard. She takes out the loaf of bread in the white plastic sack with the blue, green and red circles. She puts two slices in the toaster. Filaments flare around the bread. Bread smells filter through the kitchen over the caustic flatness of the aerosol. She takes the butter dish down and smears the butter over the toast. The smear lays a yellow color and then turns clear. Disappears into the toast.

Her diet pill runs out. The as-per-usual smooth buzzing *tic tock* runs out, leaving a hollow tube around the outer rim of her skull. She gained the weight after she woke that one night, the night she remembers as *that night* and she didn't find Roger in bed. Cherry blossoms bloomed outside and the girls had tracked them into the house. Aileen found white slips under the tables and browning in the backs of closets. She woke *that night* to a creaking noise and a tickling blossom she'd somehow sucked into her nostril. Roger's side of the bed is empty. Nightwater, her mother used to call it. Aileen didn't call it anything.

Roger didn't come back for ten minutes, twenty minutes, until in the middle of *that night* she listened and heard a sobbing somewhere in the house. She stared at the moldings around the ceiling. Roger had tacked them up, ornate leaves wrapped around berries all painted white. Between the moldings and the ceiling cobwebs collect. Can't get clean now because of the spiders. Fiddleback spiders have violins on their backs. What is the difference between a violin and a fiddle? Lay in bed. Pretend she is dead. Count Dracula will pass her up for easier prey. The light will come and she will vacuum. Spray the kitchen air with Lysol. Eat toast. A cavern of dripping stomach acid opens in her stomach, a deep gurgling pool of bile. Roger is like Orson and she is like she was when she was with Orson, she is the same and her girls are the same. It may happen all over again. Her minister, when she told him, nodded and asked her again without looking at her. He stared at the walls of his office, browned photos of fishing trips, a man wearing a life preserver and holding an eel-length trout, the livid belly the whitest streak in the photo. The minister's face dripped with yellow oil. Roger woke Aileen returning to the bedroom, pajamas bunched. His knuckles were bone white specks in the nightlight. He dressed with his back to her, beside the bed, and eased down with a contented sigh.

The yellow bus moans as it stops. The tires crush and pop the gravel. Day over.

Martha knocks open the door. Her arms full of books. Mary slips in behind her, no books, and disappears up the stairs.

"I'm home, Mom. Sitting in your spot?"

Martha lays her hand flat on the TV screen, leaving a silhouette of her palm print on the greenish bubble.

"You've been watching TV."

"I haven't."

"The TV is warm."

"I haven't been watching TV."

"It's warm."

"Are you calling your mother a liar?"

She jumps up the stairs. At the top, she stomps.

"The TV was warm, Mom."

Between four o'clock and five o'clock in October, a week before daylight saving time the light comes through the front window and glances in the right places. The light bounces through the windows, clean on this side, her side, and filthy on Roger's side, splattered with raindrops and tiny dirty circles where the dried rain left circles of coal dust. She likes to stand in the hallway and feel the light fall around her. Daylight saving time is an idiot idea. If a desperate soul wanted to change the hours they should change their own clock. It doesn't require an act of law to alter the laws of nature. She keeps her own wristwatch five minutes fast. Her wrist has no watch. Where is her watch? In the empty soap dish in the upstairs girls' bathroom where she left it to see and remind her: soap. She finds the box of spare soap bars in the hallway cupboard. She opens the new box. The bar comes out into her hand feeling waxy and smelling clean, not like Lysol but like scrubbed skin. The letters IVORY are crisp and sharp in the block of soap. The line around the soap mold still has tiny stray fibers of soap falling off. She takes it up to the girls' bathroom. She knocks. A damp towel lays bunched on the floor. She sets the soap on the counter. She rinses the soap dish. Hardened soap and filaments of hair cake the upper tray. Mucous soap-fluid fills the inner dripping trays looking like—she really shouldn't think about things like that—but it looks like a little dish of sperm. She washes it down the drain with hot water. She looks at herself in the mirror, which she didn't mean to do. She doesn't look at herself in mirrors because then she sees those wrinkles around her mouth. She sees the harsh hair that looked passable at the hairdresser but in this room with the daylight coming down through the yard and the windows Roger needs to clean; her hair looks like a Brillo pad, like bundles of wire on an SOS pad. Harum-scarum doll. Her face disappears in the weight she gained after *that night*. Eight months after her wedding day she arrived at *that night*. She eats pies and potatoes and liver and onions and this is what happens. She's always liked bread, that's her problem. *The problem with Aileen* being her favorite phrase. *The problem with* so and so and she is a so and so. So, she likes a good slice of toast, *that's her problem*. The toaster is diabolical. According to Roger, a useless invention, a result of an abundance of electricity. Too much of a good thing. She covers her toast with butter. She can have a single piece of toast. That is all she should have, but during the day, the loaf of bread slowly disappears and during the afternoon with the kids at school she'll walk down to the store and buy a new loaf. It isn't the pie or the potatoes. *The problem with* Aileen is the bread.

The bathroom is a mess. She walks down the hallway to Mary's bedroom and taps her door with her knuckles. Thinks about tapping a door with her knuckles. It has to be the right volume. She often taps too loudly. She is used to the real doors her grandfather made out of planks of wood. Had to bloody her knuckles to wake him up on a Sunday morning. These hollow doors dent if she knocks with the force an old door had to take. Don't want Mary to think she's mad. Just want her to clean the bathroom. Girls need to understand the consequences of their actions.

"Mom, what is it?"

"Dear, you left your towel in the bathroom."

"The bathroom? I'm going to get to it."

Aileen stands in the hallway, feels the sunlight on her face. The light comes down and she can see particles of dust in the air, not patterns with any kind of forethought, just eddies of air caught in the movement of the girls and herself through the house. Roger's new Dodge Dart drifts into the driveway. Four doors. A door for each person in the family he says. What about Marshall? Five of us in this family. Marshall can sit in the middle. Roger smiles. She watches him sitting in the Dodge. He looks at the house and then opens the door. Has a little trouble getting out of the car, his foot caught. He almost stumbles and turns around back to the car. He slaps the side of the car. He reaches in and pulls out his briefcase and umbrella.

When she opens the door, he bares his teeth at her. A wide, ivory swath of chipped teeth. He smells like work, smoke, rain, and graphite.

"What did you do today?"

Mary

When Mary's stepfather comes home she can hear him readjusting the car in the gravel driveway. He likes to park his car just so, not under the pine with grayish bark and bristly tufts of needles, like an entire tree full of bathroom brushes. Mary often sits in the bathroom on the toilet with the plush, yarn cover, and looks out through those needles, past the dangling black power cable, to the blue sky full of white clouds with their tops lit pastel by the setting sun. On the night of the Homecoming game, they are orange and pink and blue licorice colors. More often, though, the setting sun isn't visible. It is just a gradual, fading light in the neighborhood where Roger Carnation moved Mary's mother, Martha's brother, and older sister, Martha. Mary doesn't think of this house as her place, but as her stepfather's house. She and her sister and her brother are just staying there temporarily until they get old enough to have on their own lives. Roger Carnation is just staying there temporarily, too, waiting until they leave and he can finally have Mary's mother and any future children to himself. Roger Carnation rented the house with Mary's mother. When he first met her, they still lived in the shack Mary's actual father built on Sunset Highway. Mary's actual father wasn't allowed to see them anymore. He lost his good factory job. He was asked to leave the house by the judge. When they all lived there together as a family, with the mommy and daddy being the actual mommy and daddy, the place didn't seem like a shack. It had remained a *house* until one day sitting on the hard, pew-like court bench a judge, wearing a three-piece, brown suit and heavy black glasses, had called Mary's old home a *shack* and not a house and not a place fit to live. Mary grew up, she realized in the courtroom, in a place not fit to live. Mary doesn't know what happened to her father after he lost his job and moved out of the shack. Her mother says she wasn't allowed to have contact with him after what he'd done. You don't want to speak to an unspeakable monster like that anyway. A man like that can't be a father to you. Mary knows her mother knows what has happened to him and still sees him even though the girls are no longer allowed to see him. Marshall has seen him. He came back from visiting Mary's father with a stuffed mallard that he keeps in his bedroom. The mallard looks green but when she really looks at it she can see that the mallard isn't really green at all but a sort of black and yellow and blue with almost metallic overtones, but standing across the room it looks green. Her brother refers to this as a trick-of-the-eye. Mary likes this. If a shack is really a home, is that a trick-of-the-tongue? It's called a euphemism, or what is the opposite of that?

Roger Carnation backs up and then shoots forward, throwing gravel into the lawn, and finally he turns off the clicking car engine. Mary goes to the kitchen to help her mother pack lunch. The table has a pea green tablecloth and a white doily and mustard yellow place mats. A clock ticks on the wall. Roger Carnation and Mary's mother, Aileen, bought the new living room clock at Sears along with the other new items for the house. Aileen told Mary she wasn't used to buying a house full of things; she'd never had the chance to buy a house full of things before; she bought a lot of things she'd always wanted to have: a clothes washer and a dryer and a wall clock and a dining room table and matching chairs. Even so, Mary knows, because she isn't used to buying a lot of things at once, her mother doesn't buy a lot of the things she needs, such as spatulas, measuring bowls, or can openers. Gradually, Aileen took Mary to the store to buy the other things she did need. The three kids each had their own bedroom in the house with Roger Carnation; everything seemed new and spare to Mary.

Mary helps her mother in the kitchen as moisture begins to drip down from her shoulder blades, under her shirt. She knows Roger Carnation has entered the house without calling out and saying, "Hello, I'm home!" Instead he sneaks through the house somewhere in the four bedrooms, the two bathrooms, the upstairs common room, somewhere listening to Mary and Aileen work in the kitchen. The bedrooms aren't rooms but cages with pets in them. Martha, Mary, and Marshall feel Roger Carnation owning them and trying to train them like poodles. "Why do you wear those clothes," Roger Carnation once said to Mary, "When they make you look like a librarian?"

"I like the way librarians look."

"Librarians look like lonely, undisciplined slobs," Roger Carnation said.

Martha has already begun to escape. She is a senior

and far enough along in life, she says, that she isn't even going to go to Homecoming. All of her girlfriends say Martha will be sorry for the rest of her life. She will look back on the lost memories of her missed Homecoming with a deep and lonely sadness. "You know what they tell me, Mary?" Mary shakes her head, no. She doesn't know what they tell her. "They tell me I'll end up in some back alley knocked up and without a husband. That's how jealous some little girls are of a woman like me." Martha's boyfriend is named Clark Mackey, a red-headed man who works in insurance. He comes to the house almost every night from Seattle in his white T-Bird. He leaves his car idling in the driveway and often brings Martha's mother a small box of red cellophane-wrapped chocolates, or a loaf of freshly-baked bakery bread, or a glass vase with irises, things like that. Clark wears a blue suit and carries his fedora in his hand. He stands in the entryway while Martha finishes smearing on her makeup, shellacking her hair, finishing up all of the finish work she starts on herself as soon as she comes home from school. Clark looks at the prints on the wall for the fiftieth time and smiles at Roger Carnation until Martha comes out of the bathroom smelling like Chanel and the oil in her makeup. Mary thinks if she had a bag of popcorn with her she'd smell just like the Renton Mall. Martha leans forward and leaves a blotch of waxy makeup on Clark's cheek and they leave.

After her mother puts on her jacket, Aileen, Roger, and Mary drive down to the football stadium. The parking spot sits under a row of cottonwoods growing along the banks of the river.

"Let's look at the salmon," Mary says. She walks onto the cement bridge. The keystone on the bridge says 1921. She likes looking at the keystone because it is old and they stand on the bridge and look down into the silvery water of the Cedar River that starts near the Snoqualmie Pass. They can see the salmon moving under the churning water, five feet of rushing river. The salmon have slick green bodies and their muscles spiral them up the river. Occasionally, a dead salmon carcass drifts downstream along with the brown five-pointed leaves or the bright orange discs of alder leaves.

"It smells," Roger Carnation says.

"I like the smell," Mary says. "It smells like living things."

"It smells like dead things."

"They only die once they've done what they're supposed to do."

"It stinks like an old whore's cunt," Roger Carnation says.

"Mr. Carnation, what do you know about things like that?" Aileen says. "Mary, you didn't hear that."

"I've got ears in my head, Mom."

"Don't listen to a filthy man's mouth."

"It's not my mouth that stinks." Roger Carnation says. "How clearly do I have to say that? I don't need to apologize for the smell. It smells like dead fish. You either observe life the way it is or you bury your head in the sand."

"You need to watch your mouth around my children, Mr. Carnation. And I can assure you, for all of our sakes, we want life observed by strict rules. Without a sense of decorum we are all just savages. Do you hear me?"

"The hell I do."

"Do you hear me? Wild animals!"

"They're old enough to hear what they hear," Roger Carnation says.

"It's the least he's said in front of me, Mom," Mary says. She smiles and takes a big, showy breath of air. "Smells like an old whore's cunt to me, too."

"Don't speak like that," Aileen says. "It makes your mouth ugly."

Roger Carnation laughs. He walks toward the stadium.

"Come on, Mom," Mary says.

They sit in the bleachers. As they sit there, Mr. Carnation leans over to Mary and tells her what the passing people do for a living. "He's a carpenter. He's unhappy with his job and has a dog that is his pride and joy."

Mary doesn't like Roger Carnation presuming to know what other people do for a living as if he is such an accurate judge of character he can tell anything about them by their clothes and the way they walk. She knows how poorly he understands her or her mother or Marshall. The only one he even gets along with is Martha. "Why do you think you can make up stuff about other people's lives?" But she also thinks that in a way Roger Carnation is making up their lives. He came into her mother's life and then decided to tell them what they were. Martha is a whore and should be a housewife. Mary is the troublemaker and liar and should be a teacher because that is all teachers are good for, making trouble and lying. Marshall is full of himself and needs to go into the Army. Not good enough for the Navy, Roger said one night. "They are drafting people like you," he said to Marshall. "Best thing for someone who grew up in a shack. When you are done with high school you should enlist because then you can have some control over what they'll make you do." Marshall wants to go to college but Roger Carnation said, "Not on my dime, son. You need to make your way in the world like the rest of us."

Mary knows her mother is pregnant and she hasn't told anyone. She heard her crying in the middle of the night, saying over and over again, "How did this happen?" Mary wants to tell her that if she has sex with men like Roger Carnation that is what happens. Mary wonders if her own father is a man like Roger Carnation.

Roger Carnation tells Mary, as a bald man in a tweed suit carrying an umbrella passes, "That man is an elementary school principal." Roger Carnation goes down the line, "That man is a garbage truck driver, a welder, a butcher. That man is a fireman."

Mary doesn't believe him. Finally she says, "Look, you don't know what that man is."

The man she is pointing at has short hair and a mustache. He has on a beige sports jacket. "He's an engineer."

"You don't know that."

The coin toss. The kick. Aileen begins to yell. The rain splatters down. Even though the hood of the stadium rises up, the rain sweeps large, cold drops of water onto them. Mary gets up. "Where are you going?"

"To get some popcorn."

"Why are you getting popcorn? We brought sandwiches and coffee."

"I want to stretch my legs and I want popcorn. I have my own money." In line she finds herself behind the guy with the mustache and sports jacket.

"Excuse me, sir. Are you a fireman?"

The man turns around. He has a faint mustache and blue eyes. "What?"

"Are you a fireman?" Mary asks.

"No. I'm an engineer. An electrical engineer."

He's a double E, the same as Roger Carnation.

Martha

Martha takes her coat from the hallway closet where she left it. She only wore the Orlon Dior jacket Clark bought her when she went out with him. When she puts it on she feels the house disperse like smoke from an electric fire. The smoke is gone but the odor of the burned-wire insulation lingers. She doesn't think about the house at all, about the crooked ceilings one bit, or about the gray paint Roger Carnation used to insult the bathroom walls. She puts out of her mind for one minute the plywood truck cabin where he takes her in the middle of the night sometimes. Instead, the whole rickety mess fades out of her mind. She puts her hand in her pocket and finds ticket stubs, napkins from Seattle restaurants, and matchbooks with missing matches. Clark stands in the entryway with Roger Carnation. They discuss car engines and the Homecoming football game.

She smiles. Roger Carnation smiles.

"Good night."

Clark Mackey walks her out to the T-Bird. With a flourish, he opens her door. She transfers the soles of her shoes from the driveway to the car mat. Clark Mackey sweeps her crinoline skirt onto her seat and slams the door in two quick motions. She watches him walk around the car. He takes a cigarette out of the pack on the dashboard. He places it in the center of his lips, with a slight angle, held down by the roll of his lips. He pulls a cigarette out and offers her the filter. She draws it out as if she pulled sticks from pick-up sticks, a careful move, and then holds the cigarette in her lap and declines his offer of a light.

"You need to light it if you are going to smoke."

"I can't smoke in front of the house. Mr. Carnation would see me."

"Who?"

"Roger Carnation. My stepfather."

"You're calling him that now?"

"My mother started it."

Clark starts the car, and shifts into reverse. He throws his arm over his seat to see behind him, through the narrow, oval window. His fingers brush her hair. He hasn't cut his fingernails again and is in need of having his fingernails cut. She looks and sees he's cut himself shaving, a nasty cut under his left ear, a scab with a black, shiny surface. He also needs a haircut, and someone to politely let him know he has yellow pills of earwax visible in the cups of his ears. He guns the engine and it makes a noise like a comic book car, *vroom*, and lurches down the driveway and then backward onto the street. He turns forward, his cigarette cherry growing a little too long, and as he shifts into drive, as he guns the car forward in a sort of fluid shift of motion, the throttle forward as the car zips backward and then she settles in her seat as the car jumps down the road in the correct direction: away from the house. At the end of the block, the cigarette cherry leaves a pill of ash at the end and it falls off, scattering white flecks throughout the car.

She finds a matchbox in her pocket. The Spanish Castle. She removes a match.

"What's that?"

"Matchbook."

"I can give you a light."

"Not while you're driving."

Martha lights her cigarette. She takes a long drag, and then the dampness of the car, the somewhat battered dirtiness inside the car, the ashes on Clark's suit, don't seem to matter so much. She takes in a drag and holds the smoke in, looks at the cherry for a second. The car stops at a red light at the end of the block.

"Where are we going today?"

A black Cadillac pulls to the light and idles beside them. Three boys in tuxedos sit crammed in the front seat. One of them holds a brown paper bag and drinks from it. Behind them, three girls in pink dresses are talking and then one turns and looks at the T-Bird and looks right at Martha. She looks at Martha and her lips spread open, parting and showing a little bit of her white teeth. Her eyelashes, artificially long and spindly black, rise and quiver. Amanda Swift from homeroom. She lifts her gloved hand and forearm. "Martha!"

Martha lifts her hand. The light changes. "Please just go," she says.

"Martha who are you going to home—"

Clark ashes into the tray as he floors the pedal. The car whips forward, spins and fishtails on the gravel, jumps through the intersection, and makes Martha's stomach a little sick as it pounces over the lip of the hill and then soars toward downtown Renton.

"Where are you going?" She holds the matchbook and

flips the corner until it starts to roll. "You want to go to The Spanish Castle?"

"I'll have to drive you all of the way home."

"You aren't going to Guadalajara, are you?"

"Do you have a better choice?"

"Let's go somewhere, somewhere in Seattle."

"I don't want to have to drive all of the way back down here and then back to my room."

She waits in her seat while Clark puts on the clutch and then walks around to her side of the car and opens her door. He holds her hand. She lays her hand in his open hand and leans into him and then stands out onto the pavement, somewhat wobbly, and then he closes her door and locks it with his key and puts the key back into his pocket. She leads him across the parking lot. Straw white paper bags and cigarette butts lay in a trail against the wall. Slips of paper and yellowed strands of grass or hay. A mural of men in sombreros stand with bandoleers of ammunition X'ed across their chests. The group stands under a weeping willow that looks like a bundle of wires. The entire mural has faded in the smoke of the restaurant.

The hostess smiles at Clark. She wears black slacks and a tiny black vest and a little black hat with puffy balls hanging from the hat brim. "Two?"

"Mackey. I have a reservation," Clark says.

The hostess checks her notebook.

They can barely see anyone in the dim restaurant. Stucco walls with plants. They are seated at a table in an indoor patio with windows, skylights, and gigantic rubber tree plants. A fountain gurgles. A parrot screeches from a cage. The tables are large with brown tiles and a burning candle in a frosted brandy snifter.

"I didn't want to come here," Martha says.

"We're here now," Clark says. "You like it when we

are here. This is the only place that will let you drink margaritas."

"I want a tequila."

"Dos tequilas," Clark says when the waitress comes to the table.

"Two tequilas?" She asks. She wears a white pioneer style dress with a gigantic green parrot embroidered on it. She lays the menus, folded and creased with spots of grease and hardened refried beans, down on the table. She looks at Martha and then at Clark and smiles, and leaves.

Two women follow the hostess down the steps from the main part of the restaurant. The older one has on a short houndstooth dress and high heals and her hair permed in a thick, tall thatch of hair several years out-of-date now, a style popular two years before among models and a style Martha thought ugly at the time it was popular. Now it is just unfortunate.

"Clark? Clark Mackey? Carole Hess. I work in the office downstairs?"

"Yes?"

Carole looks at Martha and smiles. "How do you do? I know Clark from work." She looks back at Clark, "From the office Christmas party, if I remember correctly?"

"I think we were introduced there."

"Introduced is a way of putting it. Do you mind?" She sits in one of the empty chairs. Her friend sits down in the chair opposite.

Carole says, "I didn't catch your name, dear."

"Martha."

"Clark and Martha this is my friend Valerie."

"How do you do Valerie," Clark says.

The waitress comes back with the shots of tequila.

"Can I get you two ladies a drink?" Clark asks.

"I wouldn't want to intrude on your candlelit diner."

"It would be rude to say no to an offer of cerveza."

"In that case, I'll take a double scotch on the rocks."

"I'd like a margarita," Valerie says. "And a shot of tequila on the side."

"Are you going to want dinner?" The waitress sets down a basket of chips and salsa. Valerie takes a handful, breaks them into pieces, and scatters them over the table. She lays them out on her napkin.

"I'm hungry," Martha says.

"Next time you're around we'll order," Clark says to the waitress.

The two women talk to Clark about work. When Carole tells a story she leans over and lays her hand on Clark's knee. He doesn't take her hand off but leans forward, his eyes blue and glittering in the candlelight. "Do say?" And then Carole and Valerie guffaw. "You won't believe what kind of things have been going on since Randall came over from your firm. No wonder they let him go. He earns his money, he surely earns his dough, but he's gone through four secretaries in four months. And the last one was married. I'm surprised her husband didn't come in and snap his neck."

"What does the secretary's husband do?"

"Welder. He's not a big guy, and Randall is considered pretty big but not in any kind of shape and this welder could bend him over his knee and break his bones just like that. He's a short guy and when he's working in construction downtown putting together those steel frames they make the buildings out of he'll come, and he and his wife would eat in the park across the street. Randall even ate lunch with him one time."

The waitress returns and asks them whether they are ready to order. Carole looks at Martha. "You were hungry, dear?"

"I can wait until you are finished with your story."

"Why don't you order, Martha? Are you ready? I know I'm ready for another shot and a Corona."

"Another round?" The waitress asks.

"And some more chips," Valerie says.

"Does anybody want something to eat?"

"I'm fine, thanks," Carole says.

"Just another margarita and tequila for me," Valerie says. "And some more chips."

"I'll have a burrito with a side of sour cream," Martha says.

"What was I saying?" Carole asks. "That girl. Get this, instead of coming in and throwing Randall off the roof he started beating her up. She started showing up with bruises and so Randall started taking her out to lunch. Where maybe before there had perhaps been some workplace hanky-panky they started disappearing for an hour in the afternoon. And then, she showed up with a broken wrist and couldn't type so he let her go because she couldn't do the job.

"I understand he likes a good hand job more than anything else. Perhaps this is why he fired her. Come on, typing?"

Valerie laughs. "That is what he does like. Believe me. I had to cover for this woman after he fired her. I thought I was going to get bursitis."

The waitress returns with more chips and the drinks. She hands them out. Martha swallows her shot. When her burrito comes she eats it and then another round comes, and she drinks another shot. She is fuzzy around the margins.

"We've got to go," Clark finally says. He leans down and kisses Carole on the cheek and kisses Valerie on the cheek and pays the bill at the cashier's stand and they walk outside. They hear the amplified marching band playing across town at the stadium. They walk down the sidewalk, bumping into each other.

"What's wrong?"

"What do you think? You talked to those two hags instead of having dinner with me. You didn't even order food."

"What does that have to do with me?"

"You didn't even pay attention to me. Why do you even know those nasty women? And why are you talking to those nasty women in front of me?"

"You should know about me. That is part of me, that's the working world, honey."

"I don't like that part of you."

"You like money, don't you?"

"Are you paying me? Because if you are, you should know I am not that kind of woman."

"I'm sorry, sweetie." He leans against her and kisses her. "I'm not paying you." She steps back and finds herself in the nook outside of a second-hand store. It is brightly lit, and she can see the assorted junk arranged on old tables, in cases, and she goes into the store. A bell clangs. An elderly woman with cat's eye glasses sits in a stuffed chair reading a creased *Life* magazine behind the cash register, petting a cat. The woman doesn't move but smiles at them and then goes back to her magazine.

They walk through the junk store. Clark says, "I'm sorry. What can I do to make it up to you? I'll buy you something." They begin to make up a story about the stuff in their house. "I want a house," Martha says, "with a junk room."

Finally, he finds an old silver hand mirror that costs fifteen dollars. "I'll get this for you."

She doesn't want the mirror, but she wants something from him. So she says all right.

He gives it to the woman behind the counter. She wraps

it. She says it belongs to a friend of hers. A lovely woman who used to live in a house where the highway is. The junk shop proprietor has a cameo on her shirt. When she stands up the cat jumps down and looks startled. The cat takes three steps forward and then sits down and makes a jerky strike with its tongue at the base of its spine just above the tail, and then it jumps back up to all four feet and briskly walks to its water dish and takes a drink and then disappears under the heavy pieces of furniture.

They walk outside and down the block to the bridge that passes over the river next to the city library, a large, new building overlooking the river. They can smell the river a block before they arrive at the dark, gurgling water. They walk down to the trail alongside the river and sit on a bench. The river is a dark, surging flow, and they can hear it and barely see it. He kisses her, and she kisses him, and then they are kissing on the bank. He asks her whether she'll do that thing, and so she does that thing. She unzips his pants and brings her mouth down to his zipper, careful to keep the metal away from her lips. She's been cut before. Finally, he fills her mouth. She thinks about something else. She swallows it, and has the taste of the river in her mouth.

Everyone is asleep when they come back, except for her stepfather who comes out of the bedroom where Martha's mother sleeps. Her mother doesn't stir in the middle of the night, she might stir actually but she is much too warm. Her stepfather never goes to sleep. He must lay himself down at ten o'clock when everyone else sleeps, he must read the books he is always reading; he is always working on his education. He walks into the living room wearing his boxer shorts and his white T-shirt. He can't know Martha has been drinking. She tries to keep the smell of tequila to herself. She tries not to drink tequila because it smells. He intersects as she tries to make it to the stairs before him. He meets her on the first step. No one runs, just a rapid shuffle as they try to work it out. She wears her dress. She knows she smells like cigarette smoke and tequila. "You've been out drinking," he says. He can smell her. He says this not whispering but in a low voice loud enough that maybe Martha's mother can hear it if she listens, which she probably isn't because she is asleep. And even if she was awake, she wouldn't want to hear it anyway.

Martha sees him standing in the dark room. The new clock keeps time on the wall *tick tick tick* and the face of it, the gilded aluminum, reflects the field light from outside. She has had enough to drink that she is tired and wants to go to bed. She is sick really, and she doesn't want to wake anyone up. Her stomach feels queasy. If she does wake anyone up it would be her mother and she doesn't want to wake her mother, so she takes her stepfather by the hand. She reaches out and takes his hand. This is how it happened the first time. She took his hand and placed it on her breast. He is going to do it anyway and if she does it, she is in charge.

"Let me go to bed."

"Your mother is not going to like knowing you were out there with that guy doing god knows what."

"Better than inside doing god knows what."

"I'm going to tell her that you were drinking."

"Unless? Why don't you wake her up, Bob?"

"You're mother is not going to like knowing you were out there doing god knows what."

"God knows. And it surely seems as if you have some idea what I was doing, too."

"I'm going to tell her."

"Why don't you wake her up?" She puts his fingers into the top of her dress, twisting them. Martha twists until she hears him grunt. And then, she lets his fingers fall.

He runs his fingertips over her breast. She can hear his breath come out, and he makes a noise. It was mostly just the exhalation of his breath.

"Come on, then. If you don't want to wake mother up."

"I don't want to wake mother up. "

They step down the stairs. Each step creaks. They go down the steps out to the garage. They enter the camper, and the magic lantern begins to turn. She kneels on the steps and pulls his boxers down around his ankles.

She sucks on his penis. Rocks on her feet in a half crouch and damps her lips and then sucks and rocks her mouth over the shaft of his penis. She turns.

Phua. She spits onto the floor. "Go back to bed, Bob."

"Are you going to clean that up?"

"It's your mess."

When she leaves the plywood camper she realizes she's left her bag inside.

Roger

Roger Carnation swerves the Dodge over to the left side of the road. The oncoming side of the road is clear of oncoming traffic. There isn't even a parked car, although a car can always jump around the corner. Ed Wainwright down the block takes a right face at corners and speeds pell-mell down the block, not stopping for balls or toddlers or tabbies sleeping on the warm, black asphalt. Always necessary to watch out for the crazies. Roger Carnation keeps the car tires on the pavement. The tires, if they left the road, would splatter mud and gritty specks on the blue-metal door panel. He'd need to wash it off with the garden house. The green tube lies in a tight coil in the garage and had better remain in its dusty plywood box until spring, a proper time to enjoy washing the car. Roger walks feels the asphalt bite his soles, and the water sprays on his ankles, exposed by his rolled trousers rolled to a tight band across his calf. He sprays the car down and puts suds on the blue enamel car paint and looks at the reflection of clouds and telephone poles and sunlight in the bubbles. He swerves to avoid the moving bike. He doesn't ever swerve. He swerves just right to avoid mud splatters and to avoid the cyclist. Marshall rides the bike, to where Roger doesn't know. The boy constantly leaves and comes and doesn't have the sense to bring his girlfriends around for Roger to inspect, Roger suspects, because Marshall, a trombone slider and protractor manipulator, couldn't even entice sensible, ugly girls to the house. His trombone rides behind Marshall. Tufts of wild curly brown hair billow in the wind. Marshall has hair from Aileen's first husband, Orton, who no one talks about. Roger met him once. He sat at Ed's #1 wearing his gray county road crew overalls and work boots with cement and pebbles clotted to the rubberized souls when Roger and Aileen stopped for coffee. She suggested it for old times' sake, and Roger likes old-times' sakes, keeping ticket stubs and brochures and bus schedules until they turned soft and slightly green in the glove box. Orton stood away from the diner counter and introduced himself. He shook Roger Carnation's hand. He didn't look Roger in the eye. Roger looked Marshall's father right in those eyes that wouldn't look at him. Not just Marshall's father but also Martha and Mary's father. Didn't consider him really the girls' father because he was a man and passed his manner down to Marshall. The girls' straight black hair and white skin with a constellation of brown moles and curly, pubic mole hair came from their mother, as if this trait handed down from their mother made them women with heavy round waists, flat bottoms, long legs, jigging round breasts—not the limp socks or tiny mounds or triangle flaps some women carried—instead of Marshall's thick shoulders and neck and thick hair and his way of a sudden quiet laugh at Roger Carnation's expense. That is what it is, a laugh Roger Carnation paid for out of his billfold just as he pays for the jars of raspberry jam Marshall gobbles up weekly. The laugh is a hard noise like the rattle of the spoon grazing the jar's empty and sticky glass bottom. When Roger Carnation sees that smirk, he thinks, what has he just said? He hasn't said anything funny, has he? Some mannerism perhaps that Marshall thinks ridiculous? Marshall talks about how funny so-and-so is and how so-and-so is so odd. Roger Carnation knows he has an odd family and has been told by not a few people where he works (The Boeing Airplane Company, the Renton Plant) that they like working with him even if he is such an odd egg. He knows he is odd and counts himself lucky to have found a woman, even a woman already married and divorced, and triple lucky to have found not a single woman but a pack of women, count them: One, a full grown woman named Aileen, two and three, two full grown daughters (also women) variations of difference from Aileen herself. Aileen is a little worn around the edges, to be honest. She could stand to lose twenty-five pounds. Her eyes float in a dilapidated field of wrinkled skin. Where Aileen's lips are pale red, her daughters' lips have the sweet, sugary hang of Barringer Farms Jam. He is not a rich man, but he is sometimes a fortunate man.

The squat, black coffin tied to the luggage rack. That's what his trombone looks like. Marshall doesn't wave. Roger Carnation turns into the driveway. He parks in the middle. It is his driveway. When he parks he considers pulling over to one side in case someone else comes, in case, for instance the young man comes to pick up Mary. He drives a T-Bird. Roger Carnation doesn't want the T-Bird, half of a highly polished white egg to park next to the blue egg carton of his Dodge. He hopes Aileen and Mary will be ready to go. Roger will eat a sandwich in the stadium. Hazen High school, the girls' High School, plays Renton High School. Renton has Homecoming and his manager's son plays as a fullback on Renton's team and talks about how Hazen held back the whole district from playing in the triple-A league. Roger doesn't care about who wins the game, but he would like his manager to lose.

Roger Carnation closes and locks the door to the car. He has his key ready. He likes to open the door to the house as quickly as possible and then slip into the house. He never announces his arrival, but walks through the house. Whenever he comes into the house, he stands quietly in the front hallway breathing slowly. He once made it to the hallway and saw Martha naked in the mirror blow-drying her hair. The hair floated in a shaggy corona around her head, a halo of dark hair, and he saw her breasts, not the sagging breasts (not bad at her age) her mother had but still as full and mature as her mother's breasts, disc-shaped areolas with a ring of tiny bumps around them like a ring of tiny mini-nipples. The planet Saturn with its pink rings seemed feminine to him in a similar way. An unfortunate name for the planet though— but planets didn't have female names for some reason. A mistake, really. Roger stood in the hallway watching her and never said anything, but despite wanting to go right into the bathroom right then and set his briefcase on the toilet seat and put his head between her breasts he didn't do anything. Every time he comes home that is the one memory he returns to and the restraint he has placed on himself not doing anything; a true man of restraint, that is what he is; he is a brave, faithful man. There is the gurgle of water running in the bathroom. The door is closed although he knows Martha is in the shower. He eases down to the kitchen and he can hear Mary and Aileen talking about the school Mary is applying to. A pain cuts into Roger's stomach because how is he going to pay for anyone's school? He has known this family for two years; he works and is expected to be the financial bulwark for all of their dreams and aspirations? That doesn't seem likely. He is not a rich man. He puts his briefcase in his office. The drapes are closed. His coffee cup and half-eaten piece of morning toast are where he left them in his study. He hangs his mackinaw over the back of his chair and takes the morning paper and the dishes into the kitchen. On the way down the hallway he walks his special announcement walk a little louder to make sure that everyone hears him coming instead of the careful Indian-style walk he mastered at summer camp in the 1930s and perfected in the quiet winter nights when he used to sneak down and visit Jean.

"Good evening."

"You scared me. I didn't know you were home."

"How long have you been home?" Mary asks.

"Are the sandwiches ready?"

"Egg salad."

"What happened to the roast?"

"Marshall ate it."

"Marshall doesn't have a job. He's the one who deserves egg salad."

"He's anemic. Beefsteak is good for him."

"Until he gets a job and buys the meat around here. Save a little something for me, won't you dear? We don't have enough money for me to feed Marshall's gluttony."

Roger Carnation dumps the bread into the trash. He throws the paper down on top of it. He puts the lid on it and then drags the whole thing around to the side of the house where the heavy tin cans are, and he dumps the contents of the kitchen trash into the bigger trashcan. He turns over the crushed eggs, the slips of bloody butcher paper, potato cuttings, and finds a piece of paper. He pulls it out of the trash. One side has a mathematical equation. Trigonometry, not Calculus yet, and a note. Roger Carnation puts it into his pocket. He takes the bucket inside and washes his hands.

Mary sits at the kitchen table reading a book. The kitchen is empty. He looks at the light coming down through the trees behind the house into the vegetable garden. He opens the refrigerator and takes out a tomato and slices it up. He washes his hands, salts the tomato, and eats a slice while he looks at Mary. He figures she is really better looking in her way then Martha, but Martha kisses him, and there is something dangerous with Mary that he doesn't want to interfere with or get tricked into believing so he eats his tomato and looks outside. He likes the yard in the fall because there is no mowing and the grass becomes thick and green without him doing anything. Aileen comes to the kitchen wearing a twin piece.

In the stadium parking lot, they can smell the salmon in the river, so they walk over the bridge and look down and they can see the salmon swimming up from Lake Washington up the Cedar River. They look at the salmon. They are a fishy and thick and organic odor, a wonderful reek. Mary says they should just sit there and look at the salmon swim up the river. It is a much better thing than watching a stupid football game. Aileen wants to get good seats, as if there are any good seats in the entire damn building. They are as good as a pillory.

They walk across the big parking lot, pretty much empty at that end and then more and more cars. Roger circles a gigantic mud puddle with earthworms in it. Near one edge the puddle seems to drop into a deep pit of water and swirling, drowned leaves.

A heavily made-up older woman takes the tickets. She repulses Roger. She is tainted. He likes his girls pure.

Well, as pure as they are likely to be. No one is pure as the driven snow. We are born into sin. They walk through the milling crowd. The stadium is dressed with the high school colors of Hazen High. This is their homecoming game. A giant papier-mâché totem pole sheds colored tissue paper in front of the stadium. They walk around the track and then sit in the Away Side of the stadium.

Martha reads her book. Roger sits there with his hands in Aileen's hands. He figures he is doing time. Aileen will remember his hand in her hand.

Roger watches the cheerleaders. He watches them and he enjoys the flow of the game, the standing up, and raising of the crowd's voice in a large din, the bodies of the young girls getting excited and purple in the cold. Finally, the game ends. The sky is dark. He can smell the salmon more strongly in the cool, still air.

They return home. Roger feels antsy from the cheerleaders. After Aileen and he turn in, he leans over and grabs her breast. It is soft and has even more give than a bag full of air. She grunts and swats his hand. She curls into her position of defense. She won't let him do anything even though he held her hand for nearly two hours. He wanders the hall in search of a glass of water. He drinks the water down to the bottom of the glass and waits for the last drips of water to roll down the side of the glass. He knocks on the door for Mary. "Good night," he says. He talks to her about her math. He shows her the geometric proofs that he himself learned by rote many years ago. He almost leans over and tries something with her. It doesn't work because she is insensitive to these things. He leans and she shifts her weight away from him.

He waits up for Mary sitting in his rocking chair and drinks coffee. He drinks the cup and looks out at the limbs of the trees moving slightly in the breeze. Their shadows shift on the pavement. He reads the books he is required to read for his work and for his education because he always worked on his education. He gets up when he hears the T-Bird rumble away and he comes out into the living room wearing his boxer shorts and his white T-shirt. His hair is slightly mussed from lying in bed, but he doesn't need a lot of sleep, and he slept briefly from 10:30 when his new bride had put out her light until 2:30 or 3:00 depending, when Martha returns from her date with the boy in the blue suit. He intersects her crossing toward the stairs to go up to her bedroom in the attic of the house. He meets her there. She wears her dress and smells like cigarette smoke and tequila. "You've been out drinking," he says. He says this not whispering but in a low voice loud enough that maybe his new bride can hear it if she is listening, which she isn't because she is asleep.

The new clock keeps time on the wall *tick tick tick* and the face of it, the gilt aluminum, reflects the streetlight from outside.

"Let me go to bed."

"Your mother is not going to like knowing you were out there with that guy doing god knows what."

"Better inside doing god knows what."

"I'm going to tell her that you were drinking."

"Unless? Why don't you wake her up, Bob?."

"Your mother is not going to like knowing you were out there doing god knows what."

"God knows what. It seems as if you have some idea what I was doing."

"I'm going to tell her."

"Why don't you wake her up?" She puts his fingers into the top of her dress, twisting them. Martha twists until he can't help himself and he grunts. And then, she lets them fall.

He runs his fingertips over her breast. His breath comes out, and he makes a noise like *oh oh* oh.

"Come on, then. If you don't want to wake mother up."

"I don't want to wake mother up."

They step down the stairs. Each step creaks. *Creak Creak*. They walk across the damp lawn on the paving stones to the garage. They enter the camper, and he turns on the magic lantern. It begins to turn. She kneels on the steps and pulls his boxers down around his ankles.

She turns. "Phua." She spits onto the floor.

"Go back to bed old man."

"Are you going to clean that up?"

"It's your mess, Dad."

When she leaves the room, he sees that she's left her purse in the camper.

The Electric Oven Bake

Marshall

Marshall's mother made the cake from a box. The knife she used to coat the cake with chocolate, sugar, and butter frosting left swoops. The serrated edge left rows. The edge of the rows gleamed under the kitchen light bulb. In the old house, where Marshall's prior father lived, his mother also made birthday cakes. In that house, with its random heat and unexpected flurries of damp air, her cakes finished in unexpected ways. One side rose above the other. The center of the cake fell like a sinkhole. A wrecked donut. To compensate for this, Marshall's mother developed strategies to nullify the defects. She decorated the cake with frosting designs and animal shapes suggested by the cake's deformities. She covered the cake with sugar flowers and letters and rows and rows of candles. Marshall missed those cakes.

The new cakes, made in the electric oven, came from a box. The new cakes were perfect, ideal shapes. A skin of oily frosting covered the round cylinder of bready, dry sponge. Martha wrote Marshall's name on the top in her practiced calligraphic hand. This perfection stood as the cake's presentation. *Happy Birthday Marshall.* There was nothing difficult about these cakes except that it was difficult to enjoy them.

Mother presented Marshall the cake on his birthday with a ring of fifteen candles. Roger Carnation turned out the light. Marshall didn't like the light out because in the dark he couldn't see anything except the candles fluttering as Mary carried the cake from the kitchen counter, where it had cooled, to the dinner table still full of dinner plates, the milk pitcher, and the salt and pepper shakers shaped like upright eggs. All of this stuff cast sharp, wavering shadows. The cake gave off the odor of melting frosting: caramel and wax.

Marshall took in his breath.

"Make a wish!" his mother squealed.

He always forgot his wishes. He considered the thing he wanted. If he wished for it, it would make it so.

"Blow it out," Martha said. "The candles are melting all over the cake. I don't want to eat wax."

He thought about a wish. If he wished for too much it wouldn't happen, but this was his wish. He made his wish: Roger Carnation would die and leave his life insurance policy and then his mother could stay in the house and they could do what they wanted. He wished Roger Carnation would die of natural causes so that it wasn't too painful but that he'd die nonetheless. A heart attack. A massive brain hemorrhage. Something that would strike him down wherever he stood and leave him irrevocably dead. Roger Carnation stood at the side of the table half-singing "Happy Birthday." His baritone voice lay under theirs like the cool, clay bottom of a lake.

"Go on already," Martha said. "The cake is going to taste like wax."

He took another deep breath and then blew. The candles flickered and wavered then started to go out. The one closest to him flicked out and left a corkscrew of blue air. The candles snuffed around the cake until they were almost all out. The last one didn't go. He tried to direct the last of his breath at it, but he was out, there was nothing in the cavities of his lungs. If anything he'd made the last candle flame grow longer. What did that mean about his wish?

He didn't get it.

"Old man," Roger Carnation said. "He's an old man if he can't blow out fifteen candles. An old man at fifteen years of age."

"That's what happens when you really want your wish to come true," Marshall said.

"You lost it then," Martha said.

"I made a wish for us all," Marshall said.

The incandescent light came back to the exposed wreckage of dinner. Mary and Mother cleaned the table while Marshall, Roger Carnation, and Martha ate pieces of cake.

"This is so good, mother," Martha said. She ate half a slice. She pushed it away and sat in her chair looking at it. "I want more. I want to eat the whole thing. I want to eat everything in the world."

"Is there coffee?" Roger Carnation called out as if he was sitting alone without anyone in sight. He blinked and peered through a wall. "Is the coffee ready?"

"There is coffee," Mother said.

"I need a cup."

"You can get a cup as well as the next man. You can come and get a cup. I haven't even sat down yet." This was new, her defiance. Mother had begun not to do as she was told. This put Roger in a foul mood.

"I would like a cup of coffee with my cake."

"You can get a cup if you want a cup. I don't have a moment to get you a cup." Roger made noise as he moved. It came from the lower cache of his throat, disturbed, it seemed, by motion. A guttural pop came out as he stood to pour his coffee. He retuned balancing one of Mother's china cups on a china saucer. Thistles and stray green burrs curled around the bowl. A plume of steam rose from the black surface. Tucked into the base of the cup was a teaspoon and a cube of sugar. Roger Carnation usually drank his coffee black. He dropped the cup of sugar into the coffee and twirled the spoon around the edge of the china making it ring. He cut a large piece of cake and began to eat with oversized gyrations of his jaw.

Mother and Mary sat down. They brought in cups of coffee in mugs. "Why are you using china?"

"I can serve myself in what I want."

"Use a mug."

"Are you afraid I'm going to break it? Is that it?"

"Yes, I am," Mother said. "I'm afraid you are going to break it and knowing you, you will not replace it."

"Accidents happen. I can't make any promises."

"You'll buy a new one is what you'll do."

The china came from England. The best china in the world comes from England. Why doesn't the best china in the world come from China? The best of anything was a copy. The original was always too close to what people were thinking when they made it. It took a stranger to see what it was supposed to be. That was how Marshall felt. Ming vases were priceless and they were made out of porcelain and from China. If they were priceless that meant you couldn't buy them, so what use was that? The china had been Aileen's wedding present from Roger's mother. Roger's mother, who they didn't call grandma and who they hadn't seen except before the wedding when she came out to live in the study that had been turned into a bedroom by hanging a curtain across the arch. She sat in her room and read her books—leather-bound books with gold foil letters—histories of the Tribes of Cain, exegeses of the Dead Sea Scrolls, biographies of medieval popes. She bought Aileen a tea set that arrived in a crate from the United Kingdom. Someone had slapped a Union Jack seal on the package. They took out the pieces and nothing was broken or chipped, which pleased Roger's mother to no end. She saw this as a good omen for the wedding. "This is a good thing. No breaks or chips."

"Is this something your people believe?" Marshall asked her.

"My people?" she asked. "Dear boy, what do you mean by a statement like that?"

"It is a good thing, don't you think? It is clearly a good thing." Her people were not their people. He didn't know who their people were because she was nothing like Roger Carnation. She seemed misplaced as his mother, a plump, airy anglophile. Her son was an electrical engineer for nuclear subs who pretended to be a redneck sod farmer. He was thin, arid, his hair as dry as fiberglass.

"It is a good thing," she said. She agreed.

"A good thing."

Mother rarely used the china once she had it. She seemed mystified by it during the stay of Matron Carnation. Matron Carnation showed her how to use the set. They had tea. They spent the morning preparing cookies and small cakes for the tea. And then they made the tea and set the table and they ate it. They drank the tea. They were unused to anything besides the occasional early morning black coffee and the occasional soda at the drive-in and they found the sweet and full drink at once smooth and jittery, interesting and not entirely pleasant. Marshall's people were gathered at potlucks after church and trolled the table nibbling on each other's baked goods. Their people had tea but they always drank it black. Black tea seemed like really weak coffee. Matron Carnation and Mother kept saying to each other, "Over a nice cup of tea." Roger Carnation in the audience of his mother was courteous in ways that he never was otherwise. Mother, Marshall could tell, liked the power the tea and china set conferred on her. She served him his biscuits and when he asked to be excused—he asked to be excused—she denied him. "We are enjoying your company. The children, however, may go." And they went.

Mother read a book about tea. She read about the British and then decided to have her own tea one afternoon after church. She prepared cookies, shortbread, cake and cucumber sandwiches, and invited two friends from church home with her. Roger said he was busy. He changed into his overalls and work boots and drank a cup of tea standing at the side of the table and wrapped a cake in a napkin.

The library book remained open on the kitchen table, where she did all of the reading in the gap between making meals or cleaning house.

"The napkin," Mother said.

"I'll bring it back," he said.

He went outside and turned on the chainsaw and cut lumber.

He left the napkin outside on the fence beyond the garage. Marshall found it the next morning, damp and coated in grease. He took it back inside and left it in the sink in warm soapy water.

When Mother found the napkin, she wrung out the soapy water. She worked out the grease. She stood at the sink with the canola oil and scrubbed out the stain. Her elbow, always cracked and as dry as a stale cracker, ratcheted back and forth. When she was done, the entire napkin was faded but the dirt had been scoured out.

Roger Carnation said to Marshall, "I have something to say." His voice was dry and Marshall couldn't be sure what Roger had said. It was likely he had something to say. Marshall didn't know. He didn't want Roger to interrupt the moment in any case. The odor of burnt wax and wick still hung in blue wisps over the table. Marshall thought about his wish. He had made his wish, hadn't he? He could never remember while blowing if he still held his wish. It didn't make any sense to him to blow something out and at the same time make a wish which seemed to be something like sucking in a bunch of air and hoping that it changed things.

His stepfather woke his throat with phlegmatic snaps. "We are going hunting," he said. "I have some things to teach you."

He's going to learn me. He's going to make a man out of me. Marshall didn't say anything. What was there to say to Roger Carnation? Why doesn't he just say it? I'm gonna learn you. Marshall wanted his wish to manifest right then in a spurting hemorrhage that would leave Roger Carnation face first in a pool of his own fluid.

"Say thank you, father," Mother said.

"Thank you, Roger," Marshall said.

Roger grunted and ate his cake.

Marshall received the things he wanted for his birthday. *Dead Souls* by Gogol, a tin ringer for his bicycle, a miner's helmet so that he could explore the old coal mines in the forest above the house—although he didn't say that is what he wanted it for, he said he wanted it for his bicycle and so Mother got it for him thinking it would be something for safety. She found it at a second-hand store.

It worked by filling a vial with kerosene with a wick.

After he had opened his present, Roger Carnation said, "We are going hunting. You have some things to learn. I am going to take you to the Okanogan for your birthday. I'm giving you the gift of manhood."

He's going to learn me, Marshal thought.

"I don't want—"

"—Marshall, Roger is being very generous to include you. We talked about it and I think it is a good idea. You should say, thank you."

"Thank you."

"You're welcome. I understand you. You just don't understand yourself. Sometimes the best gift is one that you don't understand. We are going tomorrow for a week."

"A *week*?"

"We are going to enter the wilderness. You are going as a boy and you'll come back a man."

"I have plans. I have school. Don't you have a job?"

"We leave first thing tomorrow morning."

After the birthday, the celebrant was supposed to sit on the recliner with his gifts while everyone else cleaned up the party. He was supposed to sit there and enjoy sitting there with his new presents. Marshall sat there with Gogol. He started to read it. He didn't want to go to the Okanogan.

Roger Carnation woke him with a cup of coffee pressed to his lips. The surface scalded his lips. Marshall drank it and the coffee woke him up and kept waking him up. It was strong. At first he thought, oh that will do, I'm awake now and then he couldn't sit back down. He took his pack and Roger Carnation poured him another cup. They both climbed into the truck and it rumbled and shook. They started the long drive toward Omak.

"You're almost a man now," Roger Carnation said. "You are almost as old as you need to be to be a man at least. I don't feel sorry for you because you've had it easy. Maybe not when you lived with Orton. But now things are better for your family."

"Orton was my father."

"That man was no father to anyone."

Marshall didn't say anything. The coffee began to make him shake. It felt like his skin was shaking of its own accord, not constricting or flexing, but rumbling and moving all by itself. His stomach ached and he felt empty and light. "Are we going to eat?"

"We'll pull over at my diner in Easton," Roger Carnation said. "I expect Sally'll be working. She's the finest waitress on Sunset Highway. I heard that from a trucker last I was there. You don't tell that to her though. She heard the trucker and she poured scalding water on his hands."

"She said 'So sorry' and leaned down and kissed his hand to make it better. She kissed it knowing if he didn't put cold water on it he'd get a big old blister and she kissed it and then his hand was red and the trucker tried to appear like it didn't bother him at all. But it did.

"Her tits are completely, geometrically round," Roger Carnation said. "It is a sight to see. Worth the stop anytime. She's off limits but you can always look."

"I thought we were going to go hunting."

"I'm going to make you a man on this trip. You are going to kill an animal and fuck a woman."

"I don't know if—"

"You don't know anything. That's part of my role as your father is to get you to know some things."

"Orton was my father."

"Orton was a father to no one. As far as the world is

concerned you children were orphaned."

They drove through the dairy farms and small towns in the foothills of the mountains.

Roger Carnation pulled around logging trucks headed toward the pass and then they began the long climb up the South Fork of the Snoqualmie. The trees leaned over the car. The branches of the trees reached from one side of the highway to the other. The road traveled over the river on tall bridges. At one point the spray of a waterfall forced Roger Carnation to turn on the windshield wipers. The trees in the valley became larger the higher they climbed and then in the last climb up from the floor to the summit, the trees began to become smaller and smaller and the sides of the valley climbed steeper around them. The valley sides rose right up to towering peaks lost in the cloud cover; a gray sheet of fluffy clouds cloaked everything and they drove up finally to the summit. It was like driving through the fog. The summit was mostly a field of chipped rock, and the ski slopes were just alpine meadows. They stopped to pump gas and then drove down the other side of the mountains to the Easton, to a sprawling roadside diner.

"Is Sarah on today?" Roger asked at the front desk.

The hostess smiled and said, "Sarah is always on."

They sat at a booth in her section. They could see outside behind the place, salmon berries and the stunted mountain trees with moss hanging from the branches.

Sarah came to their table. The first thing Marshall noticed were the livid bags under her eyes. Her mascara had hardened at the ends of her eyelashes into tiny drops. Her skin wrinkled into shriveled folds at key points like the edge of a belt where the buckle sat against the leather. She wore a tight fitting Heidi style dress like Swiss Miss. The lace stretched across her very round breasts. She was short and her features seemed a little oversized for her body but small at the same time, except for the obviously female parts of her body. She had a large butt. The brachiating fingers of varicose veins covered her legs. A vessel had burst on her thigh leaving a dark, carnation-sized mark. She wore, incongruous to the rest of her outfit, white tennis shoes. They were splattered with brown and red stains. "How do you do this morning," she asked, "What can I get you?"

Roger glanced meaningfully at Marshall and then said, "We'd both like a plate of the Mountain Breakfast, OJ, and coffee."

When she walked away, Roger said, "I forget. How can I forget the caboose?"

She stopped and then looked back at the table.

When she returned to the table, she leaned down close to Marshall. "Can I get you anything else, honey?"

"No. Thank you."

"Killing is a responsibility," Roger said. "You can kill irresponsibly. A bullet can wound an animal in a way that won't bring it down and it will go out into the wild with a mortal weakness and then die. You won't be able to follow. It will die and then the meat will rot. It will suffer in its dying. When you kill you must do so as to cause no pain. Kill the animal instantly.

"The meat of a game animal is better than the meat of animals we buy in the store. Because it feeds on wild grasses, moss, it has different nutrients. We are what we eat, and the animal is what it eats, and so the chain goes on. I want to eat something that has grown and lived in the world where I live. That's why I don't buy canned meat. Who knows where it has come from?

"Fucking is a responsibility too.

"Does that word bother you?

"Would you prefer *making love?*

"*Making love* has little to do with fucking. Fucking is its own thing. Some women like to fuck and some don't. Some women have to be trained to fuck and once they are trained to fuck they are good at fucking. Marriage is generally about other things and it is rarely about fucking. It is about making love and now that is related to fucking but fucking and making love are two different things. I can fuck a woman I do not love. Fucking is about as far removed from love as shitting is from eating a good meal. It's the same stuff coming in and going out and you aren't about to confuse them.

"The use of a whore is twofold. One, you pay cash instead of taking on the responsibility of fucking. That is why they charge in the first place. You are responsible for paying and treating a whore with kindness and respect. You are not paying so that you can abuse them. Second, a whore is unlike a woman who wants to make love. A whore fucks. Getting away from making love is important. You'll hear from a broad who wants to make love when you are fucking her that she doesn't like to have sex, that it is an obligation, that it is a chore. That's no good. It's a chore to a married woman. But with a whore of course it's more than a chore. It is her profession. It's a job. They get it done right the first time.

"We all have to do things we don't like in order to get the things we do like generally for someone who has power over us, be he our father, teacher, boss, sergeant; the entire ball of wax is a series of trade-offs. We all need to operate in our own self-interest and as well as we can to get what we need. No one knows what we need more than we know what we need and so it is vital that you act in the most directly self-serving way possible, otherwise—"

"—otherwise what?"

"We don't get what we require. To be a man you have to: one, know what you want; two, understand the cost and assess it using a true cost/value analysis if it is something you can afford. Some things you want just aren't worth it. And some things are.

"Now that waitress back there didn't think you were all that bad. She thought you were young and you are just a boy and being just a boy means that some kind of women, the kind of women we are going to encounter on this trip, they are going to want to show you the way over because they know a boy like you is going to remember them and it is a way for them to make the crossover to something that will probably outlive them. How long do you think an Omak whore is going to live? This truck is probably going to last longer than she is going to last, what with the grain alcohol and the wild ass backwoods freaks she has to fuck in the off season to make ends meet. A young fella like you is ripe and ready, in addition to the fact that she knows she's going to make an impression.

"Open the glove box," he said.

Marshall opened the glove box. Like everything in the truck and camper it was neatly packed.

"Pull out the map," he said.

The map had something heavy wrapped in it. A silver flask with a mermaid stamped into the front of it. Someone had painted the mermaid's breast red with enamel paint.

"My flask from the war," he said. "Painted the tits red so I knew it was mine. Has my name in the bottom as well." Marshall turned it over and read Carnation's name written in a shaky cursive script. The enamel had started to flake.

"Put the map back."

Marshall folded the map and put it back and carefully arranged everything so that it looked right.

"That's right," Roger Carnation said. "You're learning

how I like things. If you bring something down then you can have a go with her."

"I don't want to."

"You want to even if you don't know you want to. I always knew I wanted to ever since I was a little boy. I was five years old and I wanted to bone my sister. Just drag her to the hay barn and throw her in there and have at her. She was seven so she was big enough that she would kick the shit out of me if I tried. First time I did it with a woman I was nine years old. I guess that is pretty young. It was my cousin who was sixteen years old. She saw me looking at her and then she said to me what are you looking at and I am looking—"

"Your cousin—"

"Don't take that tone up with me here. Shit, Marshall, I'm 45 years old. I have seen some shit in my life that would make your eyes leak blood." Marshall peeled a piece of the old enamel paint from the Carnation painted on the bottom of the flask. His thumb lifted the leg of the terminal "n," making it an r: Carnatior. The red fleck of paint clung to Marshall's thumbnail.

"Take the cap off the flask."

Marshall pulled the cap and it didn't come off. He unscrewed it. The cap was held with a chain. The plug popped and released an odor, chemical, sweet, floor cleaner.

"Let me have it."

"You're driving."

"Fuck n'shit. Let me have it."

"Not while you're driving."

"This is my truck."

"This is my birthday trip. I want to see my next one."

"Fuck n'shit, are you still a fucking boy? Give me the flask."

Marshall scooted against the side of the door. Roger reached over and socked Marshall until he was pressed against the door. The door clicked and then opened. The cool air rushed into the cabin. Marshall jerked against his seat belt and his right leg flung out of the car kicking the door open. He could see the rushing highway cement and the gravel on the side of the road. Roger only had one hand on the wheel. The truck skidded to the other side, onto the shoulder kicking up a cloud of dust and gravel, and jerking Marshall back into his seat. Roger held the flask in has hand. "Don't defy me, punk."

He took a drink and then he howled, "Fuck n'shit!" He wiped his lip with his wrist.

"Take a drink. But you give it back to me."

"Just don't drive us off the road."

Roger Carnation swerved the truck into the shoulder and low laying branches glanced across the roof.

Marshall took a sip and at first he couldn't tell what it was and then it was just like putting his mouth over the hole of a gas tank, only he had the fluid going into his throat. It was like sucking a straw stuck into a tin canister of lighter fluid. He tried to get the taste out of his mouth. He spit over the glove box. A fine spray. Mostly cough.

Roger Carnation took the flask from him and looked at the moonshine dripping down the glove box. "Lick it off."

"No."

"Lick it off. Don't try me, Marshall. You lick that off until you learn better."

A bundle of pressure built up behind Marshall's eyes, in the space behind his nose and cheeks. He licked it off.

Roger Carnation handed him the flask again. "Take another drink. If you spit it out, you'll lick it off again. You need to learn to do this."

Marshall felt Carnation was right. He swallowed and even though it burned and he felt like it was going to just float out on its own anyway he kept it down.

In the drive from Snoqualmie Pass into Eastern Washington, they drove through smaller trees, ponderosa pines. Unlike the dense forests on the damp side of the mountains, here the forests were sparse with fields of pine needles and late seasonal flowers between the trees. They could see the roll of the hills up to short peaks faced with cliffs. The cliffs were gray and blue in the early morning light. The moonshine, the gasoline, or whatever it was—rotgut—burned in Marshall's stomach and spread warmth from his burning stomach out to his limbs. For a second he stopped even hearing Roger Carnation talking. He couldn't hear anything that Roger Carnation was saying. Roger Carnation kept talking and Marshall could hear him talking but he didn't know what to make of it. He just listened to him and put his head against the seat. It wasn't a bad feeling either. He did feel sick. However, it wasn't a bad feeling. He could feel the fabric of his cuffs but then couldn't feel the fabric in the arm. If he didn't keep his eye mostly on the center of the road he became confused by the patterns in the highway. The asphalt was abraded by the passage of trucks with chains. The surface cracked where the roadbed settled. The highway department patched the cracks, leaving calligraphic patterns of the tar. The pattern rolling under the car settled his stomach and smoothed the feeling in his body.

"You aren't listening are you, son?"

"I'm not your son."

"A turn of phrase."

"Well, don't turn that phrase on me."

"You aren't feeling well, are you, son?"

"I'm not your son."

"Marshall, do you need me to pull over. Do you need some fresh air?"

"I'm all right as long as we keep moving. I just can't talk."

They drove in silence. Gradually the trees fell away to sagebrush and weathered fences. Roger turned off the main highway and headed North on a two-lane highway toward Chelan. It passed back into the forest and then into the prairie. The mountains rose up now to the west of them, massive snowbound peaks that were stark silver and white against the cyan of the sky. Marshall didn't know these mountains. The ridges, he thought, were kind of like enzyme shapes. He was unfamiliar with them, and so they had made him even sicker.

In the early afternoon, they came to the tiny town of Chelan. The lake curled into the faint bluish mountains, the lake and mountains just went on and disappeared into the distance. It was warm out now. When they stopped there was dust in the parking lot. The place was quiet except for the click and clatter of chains, barbwire, and loose gutters.

"I'd like me a place here. Everyone has a place here because it is a nice place but you could go far up the lake and then you are here and not here. You could come down here to get some coffee and bacon if you wanted. Or you could just set out from your door and you'd be in the wilderness."

Marshall walked out to the pier. They could see a sailboat in the distance. It was manned, he could see, by young men, boys maybe, in blue and white striped sweaters. He could hear then the sound of them coming across the water. They were laughing and then shouting. The boat's sail went slack and then they managed to turn it and the boat filled with wind and began to race up the lake into the bluish haze.

"Your stomach settled enough to eat?"

They went into the Chelan Diner. There was an older couple sitting at a table with the view of the lake. The waitress came and she was beautiful. She wore a white apron and black blouse and skirt. She had long brown hair that almost seemed translucent in the light coming off the lake; it caught silver and then gold light. She had a short mouth with full, almost overflowing lips. She glanced at Roger and Marshall and smiled. When she smiled a tiny mole just below her left eye moved and then settled and this mole drew attention to the smooth, buttery color of her skin. "Lunch?" she asked them.

Marshall waited for Roger to do something but Roger seemed flummoxed by the appearance of the waitress. He stared at her and began to fumble for something in his back pocket. For an instant Marshall could see him for the old man he would become, frail and spent. He didn't have pity for this sudden vision of a powerless Roger Carnation. He was satisfied.

"Yes. Just us," Marshall said. "If we could sit by the window."

"Don't know if there is room," she said.

"Well, wherever is fine," Marshall said.

"I'm joking with you," she said. She sat them at the other side of the diner from the older couple. They glanced at Marshall and Roger Carnation. Roger Carnation still hadn't said anything.

As his silence grew Marshall began to dread what he was going to say. He was going to say something and he didn't want to hear it.

Finally, he said it. "We came to the right place."

"What are you going to have for lunch?" Marshall asked.

"You can have whatever you want," Roger Carnation said. "It is your holiday."

Roger Carnation didn't look or speak again while the waitress was there. Marshall ordered for both of them and Roger Carnation gradually stopped speaking at all.

They chewed their food and drank their coffee and looked out at the lake, the clouds on the horizon, the emptiness of the world.

As the sun began to set, they drove up a logging road and through a rapidly moving stream and then finally to a dead-end spur. Roger Carnation stopped the truck and backed against a steep slope. They got out of the truck. He ordered Marshall around as they set up the camp in the failing light. They set up a tarp supported by three poles near the tent. They found old stones in an empty fire pit. Roger drew a circle and handed Marshall the collapsible shovel to dig down for the fir pit. Marshall held the dented, metal object. He pulled on one edge and the thing seemed to be jammed together. He stepped on a lever and nothing happened. Roger grabbed the shovel. Roger struck the handle with the heel of his hand. The shovel snapped open. Marshall couldn't see how he'd done that. Roger edged the circle with stones. In the dark, they stumbled through the forest to gather armfuls of fallen branches.

Marshall stood in the dark forest. He didn't know where he was. Was he in the Okanagan? Is that where he was? He didn't know he was way out somewhere and he didn't know where and he had an armload of twigs in the almost failed light. He thought that once they built the fire the fire would keep Roger Carnation from talking too much. There would be the fire to look at, too. He could look at the fire and then fall asleep. This wouldn't be such a bad thing. He was getting to know Roger Carnation a little bit better. He wasn't growing to like his stepfather. He did look forward to drinking a little bit more of the moonshine before going to bed.

When he returned to the truck he could hear another vehicle coming through the forest. He saw the lights of the other vehicle flashing down the road. He waited for the thing to drive past. It was a truck with a wooden shed nailed onto the back. Instead of driving past, though, the truck pulled up to the Ford. He could hear the voices and then laughing and then Roger Carnation saying it is about fucking time you arrived. "I thought we were late. And here you are coming in this late. I'd have spent the night in a hotel. But you knew I'd have the base camp set up if you got here this late."

"Marshall! Marshall, come out of the woods and stop doing whatever it is you are doing out there in the woods, you damn pecker wood. I want you to meet my hunting buddies, Ernest Womack and Philip Keene."

Marshall dropped his pile of wood and the two men stood in front of their truck. The engine still idled and the headlights shown into their camp, showing how dismal the situation was, really, a tarp over a bed of pine needles. The fire blazed moderately well, but the rest of the camp was just a haphazard collection of things they'd removed from the truck. The men slouched. They had stubble in various levels of growth. They didn't look remarkably well. Their skin was yellow and covered with red splotches, mosquito bites or irritation from the camp smoke. They wore hunting caps. One wore a fedora-style cap with a feather sticking out of the brim. The other wore a duck hunters cap over his ears. They wore plaid and rubberized hip waders. "Well look at this, if it isn't the young man of the family. We've heard so much about you."

They came forward and socked Marshall in the shoulder. "You play in the band, don't you?"

"Yes I do."

"We've heard that you do. Roger says you play the

trombone. He says you play excellently. Very well, actually."

"He also says," the other one said, "you can't hunt."

"That's all right. We are here to help you."

"That very nice of you," Marshall said.

He unloaded his load of sticks. "I'm just gathering wood before it gets dark."

"It is dark," Ernest said. "It is pitch black."

"Your wood hunt is finished," Keene said. "You are done unless you have some kind of way of seeing in the dark that I don't know about."

Roger Carnation came back with his flask. "I brought the stuff."

"I have the meat," Ernest said. "We brought it in an icebox."

After that they had parked with much back-and-forthing and then placing rocks under the tires of the car.

They brought out the icebox and then a case of Rainier Beer and set these beside the fire. They took out a large metal plate and placed this over an edge of the fire pit and then stuffed the area below it with twigs. It began to burn. They unwrapped pieces of meat from brown butcher paper. "Last season's kill, brother. We eat last seasons kill to get ready for the next season." And then they threw four oblong objects wrapped in foil into the ashes beside the stove. "Potatoes."

It was too dark to really see if they were cooking well. They had a Coleman lantern set up on the icebox next to the stove.

The smell of the meat frying and then burning a little struck Marshall as barbaric and also as something pleasant, to be out in the forest with no one around them except these three guys and then miles of forest and somewhere out there even more meat for them to get in the morning. While waiting for the venison to cook,

Marshall, Ernest, and Roger Carnation sat by the fire where it was too hot and drank beer. They tossed their empties into the middle of the pit.

Then Keene served the steaks and with potatoes and pats of butter like you'd get at a dinner. "This is the life," Roger Carnation said. "This is the fucking life." They passed around the salt and peppershakers, lifted from a diner. Marshall had eaten venison before and it was always made plain to him by his father or stepfather that this was how meat was supposed to taste. This is the animal that eats naturally and when we eat from it, we too are eating naturally. This was how it was supposed to taste and he didn't really like the taste, not because it was different or gamey although he'd never really thought the meat tasted that much different from beef or even chicken. It was meat and his mother, who had prepared the meat in both cases, was a careful and deliberate cook with meat. The difference was the reverence he was supposed to pay to the cut of meat because it had come from an animal that his father or stepfather had killed and this somehow infused the meat with a spice. The hunters groaned as they ate the somewhat tough steak with perhaps a little bit of freezer burn. They muttered how good it was and if they could just leave their respective homes and live here and like this all year long then they would. But September and October only come once a year, the peak of the season, and the season is overripe as it is and it could snow any day, and who wanted to live in the wilderness when it snowed? You needed a house for the snow, a fireplace, a place to hang your damp clothes, a spot to put your wife's ass when you were done with it.

Keene talked about the hot springs in the Olympic Mountains. He'd been there over the winter, the next trip over last season's hunting trip, and that was a place where you could winter in the mountains. "I had a cabin, but you could see how you could find a big old cedar tree, something with a lot of branches and it would be like a gigantic natural teepee. There is enough room under one of those things that you could lay down in your sleeping bag and build a chimney and be set."

"That's still a kind of house."

"Not really, because you're looking at a few hours work and it'll last during the height of the winter. The problem with those kinds of things though is that it depends on the real cold. As soon as it starts to get warm the entire forest turns into mud. You've been out in the spring as the snow is melting. That is the worst time of year. But in the winter, it would work fine. Shovel out the space under the tree. Start a fire and when you need to get really warm go down to the hot springs and climb in. Nothing like sitting out in the snow with snow and drizzle falling down and you're in water so hot your skin turns white."

The beer was inside Marshall now. He'd had a few of the beers. He was drunk but in a way he'd never been drunk before and he thought part of it was being out in the forest and not sure where he was going to sleep and if he was even going to be comfortable and part of it was having to listen to these two men who didn't know what they were talking about and it was like listening to the tap drip, it was like listening to the branches move and rustle outside of his bedroom window and his having to pay attention and act like it was intelligent and deliberate conversation when really it was just a product of something else—in this way he sort of envied them because they were natural products, unselfconscious, even pure in a way. They didn't have any indecision about who they were or what they were going to say. And so addressing their secret goals and dreams they had nothing to hold them back really. It wasn't like they actually thought they were going to live in the forest because a goal or a dream for them was purely metaphorical. It was something they wished to happen which meant that it was something that would not happen. A metaphor is something that is not. And for them a goal was something they would like to happen but would not. If it was going to happen, it wouldn't be a goal but inevitable, and then like death or waking up to go to work, there would be no reason to think about it. In addressing their improbable goals they slipped into fantasy—not full-on fantasy but transforming and thereby focusing on the reality of their presence in the forest which would inevitably end in the purely metaphorical proposition of what if they could stay out in the forest forever?

"It's not bad here," Roger Carnation, said. "But I like my line of work."

"I hate my fucking job, man. If I found a huge gold nugget, I'd say see you boys later. I am going to the woods."

"You'd stay at your job?"

"I have no complaints is what I'm saying. I build something I love, submarines. I have two lovely daughters and soon my stepson will be a man. I'm doing my duty for this country and this boy is what I'm saying. Things are good for me. I'm not about to wreck anything."

"You aren't a man yet?"

"I don't even know what that means," Marshall said. "I'm fifteen. I turned fifteen last week. That's how old I am."

"I had my first job when I was fourteen," Keene said. "First job makes a man."

"I grew up on a farm," Roger Carnation said. "There was no luxury of being a child. There was no luxury of a first fucking job. I was born doing my chores and then one day when I was younger than Marshall is now I stopped doing what I had to be doing and it occurred to me that if I stopped doing what I was doing that the farm would stop doing what it was doing and the livestock would starve, the crops would wither, and we wouldn't be making a living. We'd fucking starve. I hadn't thought about it before and as soon as I did, that was it. I wasn't a man, I guess, but I wasn't a boy anymore. We didn't have this phrase, teenager, then. What was a teenager?"

"No one fucking knew what a teenager was."

"Aren't you drinking beer with us?" Ernest said. "Aren't you out here in the forest enjoying the manly life?"

"Yes. That's Roger Carnation's gift to me. Manhood for my fifteenth birthday."

"Shit man," Keene said. "You can't give that as a gift. You've got to earn it."

"A gift like that you can't even take back to the store. Manhood is a fucking curse," Ernest said. "Who in the hell wouldn't want to be a kid their entire damn life? No real responsibilities. If you do something bad, it's not your fault because you're only a kid."

"That's the issue, ain't it," Roger Carnation said. "Responsibility. That is all that separates a man from a boy and nothing more."

"So you are giving me the gift of responsibility?" Marshall asked.

"You don't even know what I'm giving you," Roger said. "You won't know until you've had it."

"The burden of manhood."

"You could say it that way."

"That sounds like a curse, not a gift," Marshall said. "Thanks a lot."

They started to laugh.

"This kid is all right," Ernest said. "This kid is just fine. Why does he need to be man?"

"He ceased to be a child the day his father turned his

back on his own kin," Roger Carnation said. "The day his father was exiled from his home."

"My father didn't leave because he wanted to leave."

"We don't want to open that can of worms," Roger Carnation said. "Let's just say he took liberties that a man should not take. He violated his responsibility."

"Are you my father?"

"I'm not your father. I'm of no relation aside from marriage to your mother to you or your sisters. And in this day and age that hardly elevates me above the status of a stranger."

Ernest and Keene began to clear the plates.

"There are things that are none of your business," Roger Carnation said. "There are things that are private. When you are a man you will understand."

"Why are we here if you aren't my father?"

"You are a boy under my roof. There is no one else. That is my obligation."

"I never wanted to be anyone's obligation."

"You are more than an obligation to me, Marshall. You're a burden."

"What about Martha?"

"My duty manifests itself just as it has with you. I'm not a father to you all. I'm a stepfather. What is a stepfather? Stepmother's always the one who makes the kids do the chores. Stepmother's the one who leaves the kids under the trees to be eaten by witches. Who knows what I am? I'm doing what I need to do."

"You are doing what you want to do."

"Believe me when I tell you this, you little shit—why do you have to push this far? There ain't nothing about you or your sisters that make any of my wish lists."

Marshall stood up. "I don't know what I'm doing out here."

"You're out here to shoot an animal and earn your reward."

"What's that going to be?"

Ernest started to chuckle. "You'll see. Well, you'll see if you make it."

"Is this like some kind of secret club thing? A fraternal organization?"

"I like that," Ernest said. "I like that a lot. We're all fucking brothers."

Marshall woke hours before dawn. The tent had much more room than he or Roger Carnation needed. Roger Carnation slept on the other side of the tent near the slope of the tent, side down to the canvas. They both slept on their sleeping bags on blankets and then a rubberized mat on the ground. It was comfortable, but Marshall woke and realized he could hear something dropping through the forest. There were ticks and pops and then after a while he could hear a gurgling noise. The silence before the gurgling noise was what he woke him up. Marshall put on his jacket and slipped on his unlaced boots and stood in the darkness beside the tent. Rain fell in the forest around the tent. It was dark and he couldn't see anything but he could hear the rain coming down through the branches. He was awake now and went back into the tent and climbed into his sleeping bag, still warm from his body. He tried to put himself back to sleep because he'd be tired in the morning if he didn't sleep but even with his eyes closed he could only stay awake and hear the noise of the rain.

Roger Carnation woke sometime later, then. Marshall wasn't sure how long he'd lain in the darkness waiting for him to wake up and when he woke up, Marshall wanted him to go back to sleep. It was too soon for him to wake up.

Roger Carnation dressed in the tent, hunched over, and then he put on his boots and went outside. Marshall could hear him starting the fire and the noise of that woke Ernest and Keene. "Hey buddy."

"Get the coffee going."

They made breakfast and then Marshall climbed out of the tent and laced his boots. There was a little bit of light now from the fire and it burned despite the steady fall of rain. It wasn't a heavy rain, but already the mostly dry stream bed filled with running water.

"Bad weather for hunting. The gear'll get wet."

"It's just a morning rain," Roger Carnation said. "It'll wash everything off. It's good luck."

"Who thinks rain is good luck?"

"Natives thought it was good luck."

"Not in these parts they didn't."

"It's good luck, all right."

"What do you think, son?" Keene asked Marshall.

"I just want a cup of coffee," Marshall said.

"He's learning."

"Coming up," Ernest said. "It'll be a minute. Water just has to get hot."

They drank their coffee and ate fried eggs and ham. And then Marshall scoured out the pans with gravel from the stream. They locked everything down. It was still too early for the light. They lit their flashlights and set out on foot, Roger and Marshall headed up the road and into the hills, Ernest and Keene down the stream to a meadow they thought a good place.

"The deer climb hills."

"Do you know where the truck is?" Roger asked Marshall. "Can you find your way back?"

Marshall took out his compass. He could read the

compass, but he wasn't sure where the truck was or where he would be. "You need a map," Roger Carnation said. He took out his map and they unwrapped it. He shook it out, and then held the surface up to the early morning light. "Can you find where we are?"

Marshall found the valley and the marked stream and then he pointed it out. "Good, you can read a map." Roger Carnation started to walk without another word. He walked into the forest leaving Marshall with the map. Marshall watched him go. Water dripped from the trees.

Marshall liked the sense of being by himself. He listened for the thrashing of Roger Carnation passing through the branches and the ground cover, but he didn't hear anything. He began to walk up the hill toward the ridge-line. He spent an hour climbing and as he made his way toward the top of the ridge, daylight began to filter through the clouds. The rain stopped. The hills around the ridge were damp. The clouds broke. Sunlight caught the glistening ground. At the top of the ridge, Marshall found a trail, and he followed it and stopped when he came to a pile of deer droppings. He couldn't tell how old they were. Near the summit of the hill, the trees thinned, and there was a meadow. From the meadow he could see the next ridge and down into the next valley, a steep drop straight down. Marshall found a pile of rocks to sit on, and then he just sat for most of the day. Despite the early rain, the morning turned blue. The sun still sat concealed behind the billowing white clouds. Large parts of the sky fell away to a solid, unmarked blue. The forest around him made ticks, pops, and repeated dripping echoes. Eventually the clouds grew back over the sky and sealed the spots of blue. A herd of deer passed over the lip of the hill without a noise. They passed over the edge of the ridge and fell into the valley. Marshall fumbled with the Winchester. He brought it up and they were gone. He sat back into the rocks with the rifle pointed at the trail. He had his finger on the trigger. Behind the herd an enormous buck tumbled up the slope like reverse gravity. Marshall shot it. He hardly realized he'd pulled the trigger until the rifle threw itself against his shoulder. He saw the animal fall upward until it was in his line of site. He aimed for the animal's eyes and fired as quickly as it appeared. He was afraid it would fall past his sites. He realized when he fired he was doing something he didn't feel he should be doing, that he was trying to outshine the animal. He pulled the trigger of his tool. The cool, sleek barrel pushed a tiny piece of metal into the animal's skull. The bullet wailed. The forest filled with the odor of burned powder. After he fired there was a moment when he didn't see anything. It didn't look like he hit the animal and it didn't even look like the animal noticed that it had been fired on. A splotch appeared just above the animal's eyes. The pupils rolled white. The buck kept moving through space. It had been flying up from the bottom of the hill and then it passed into the meadow and rolled. Everything that was alive about the animal was gone. The flowing flex of its muscles, the nervous tick of its tail, the tilt of its ears dissipated. It was just bone and muddy fur and as limp as warm grapes and meat. Its horns had snapped off. The animal's neck turned like an elbow.

The fur felt like a rabbit's foot. The hide was bristly and very warm. He could move the body but trying to lift the body was a different thing altogether. He tried to move the body, but the body just shifted as he pushed it. The taut fur of the buck was speckled with ivory. He slipped under the bulk of the stag and then he pulled the chest up from the ground. He didn't have enough strength to just pick it up. He rolled it up onto his back when he squatted down. He pulled the legs and then slid his head under it and then he had the animal on his shoulders. He draped it across his back and stood in a squat with the center of the animal on his shoulders. The heavy flanks trailed off. Fluid from the wound in the head of the animal ran down Marshall's back. It came out warm and dripped away cold. He took a step and wanted to let the animal down, but after several steps he could anticipate the weight and he didn't want to start over again. He took several more steps and then walked for as long he could stand it. He was about halfway down the ridge. He wasn't sure then where he was. He couldn't carry the weight anymore. His legs hurt. He lowered the animal down; he tried not to drop it. The flesh would bruise like a banana if he dropped it. It was something he owned now. It was a living thing and now he owned the bones, the fur, the meat, the blood of the animal because it was dead. He killed it and peeled away the living part of the animal and he took the dead part of the animal, the body. He took something that was living and then he killed it and made it a dead thing and he owned the dead thing and the living thing was gone. He had destroyed the living thing in the animal. Marshall had killed something as large as the buck with something as small as the bullet. Marshall wanted to kill more things. He wanted to experience the transformation promised to him. He had not understood the murderous impulse of his friends who shoot down starlings, squirrels, and rats at the dump with their BB guns. They said they were going to go to the dump and meant they were going to kill something. He didn't want any part of anyone going somewhere to kill something. He understood now why they liked to do it.

He could, finally, lift the body. The animal's legs draped across his back. He walked down the ridge for about half a mile, until he couldn't carry the buck anymore. Blood and burrs of shed fur coated his shoulders. Blood dripped down Marshall's sides. He decided he would go to the camp and get some help in carrying the body back.

He knew he was at the top of the ridge, but he wasn't sure which ridge. It was the first ridge, he thought, but in the morning before he was awake and he was just walking, he wasn't sure if he came over one ridge or three. He was just working his way out into the woods.

He took out his map and tried to figure it out. He would just keep in mind where he was coming from and he would be able to lead them back.

It was in the late afternoon and he had several hours before it was dark. He headed down the slope until he came to a stream. He remembered then coming up the ridge to this stream. He looked back behind him and tried to remember where he'd left the buck. He walked back up to the top of the ridge and he could see smoke coming up from the valley, but he couldn't tell where the smoke was coming from. He walked down the ridge until he came to the road. At the top of the ridge it was still daylight, but as soon as he came down to the road on the valley floor it was dark. The light was still up on the ridge top. Marshall walked along the road and came back into the camp.

"Whoa, look at you," Ernest said.

"What happened to you," Keene asked. "All covered in blood. Is that your blood?"

"It's my kill," Marshall said. "I killed an animal."

"Well where is it?" Roger Carnation asked. His voice carried a thick, barking timber and echoed in the narrow valley.

Two gutted deer hung from a line strung between two trees. Marshall wondered whose deer they were.

He handed the horns to Roger Carnation. "You took off the horns?"

"They broke off."

"That is your blood," Roger Carnation said. "That

is your blood and you found these horns. You were supposed to bring a deer, not some old horns."

"Naw, man," Keene said. "These horns came off a live deer."

"Well where is it?"

"I couldn't carry it," Marshall said.

He led them down the road and realized he should have marked where he went over the hill. He knew he couldn't turn around or they would get impatient with him. It was beginning to get dark. He stepped into the trees and they could hardly see where they were going and they walked up the hill and at the ridge top he climbed down. "Hell, no, man. How far in the fuck is this animal? It is getting dark."

"We are almost there," Marshall said.

They crossed the stream and he started to walk up into the forest. It was on this ridge, but he wasn't sure how far up or how far down the ridge. They circled around in the failing light and then finally he stopped. "It is on this ridge."

"That isn't close enough," Roger Carnation said. "It needs to be closer than that."

"I don't know. It's on this ridge."

"Where?"

"I don't know."

They went back to the camp.

"Maybe your son is a liar?"

"He's not my son. He's my wife's son."

"That makes him your son."

"First husband's son. She is remarried to me."

They tried to follow Marshall's path through the woods. When they set off, the sun had already cleared the branches. After twenty minutes of following Keane through the woods, it became so dark they could only see the white lining of their jackets, the silver lines of the rifle barrels, the reflector discs they wore on their jackets to keep them from shooting each other. The woods became completely dark. Ernest lit his flashlight, a yellow arc of light that only made the darkness that much darker in contrast. "This light won't last more than twenty minutes," Ernest said. "We need to turn back."

"He should stay here," Carnation said. "The kid should stay here until he finds his kill. You don't leave a kill in the forest. That's one of those things that you think you don't have to tell a kid."

"He couldn't carry it," Keane said. "We should have had a plan for him if he did kill something. We thought he couldn't do it. Hell, I was a numb nuts my first six years in the woods."

"Can't you remember where it was?" Carnation asked.

"I can't see anything. I don't even know where I'm at now."

"We need to turn back," Ernest said.

"You need to find that deer," Carnation said. "Don't come back to camp until you have it."

"He can wait until tomorrow."

"Coyotes will get to it tonight if he doesn't find it now."

"I don't like leaving him out here. He is your responsibility."

"He needs to find it."

They stood around Marshall.

"You get lost, son, in the morning follow the stream downhill and you'll come to the road. Either way you go you'll come to a store," Keane said.

"You aren't leaving me out here."

"You sure as hell aren't coming back to camp without your kill," Carnation said.

"But even if I find it, how will I carry it home?"

"That's not really for us to figure out," Carnation said. "You figure it out with the thought that you have to get that meat back to camp."

They left Marshall standing under a stand of pine trees. He watched the light go away. They didn't talk as they left. They didn't even laugh. Marshall wondered if they had gone even too far for them. He thought about just finding a place to sleep and then in the morning walking out of the woods. He could do that. He sat against the side of a pine tree. It smelled of pitch and pine needles. He couldn't see anything in the woods there and finally drifted off to sleep. He woke with a sharp pain in his lower back from the roots of the tree pressing into flesh. He lifted himself by the sides of the tree.

He remembered he had his birthday present in his bag. He found the miner's helmet Mother had given him wrapped in newsprint. He found his lighter and lit the wick. Around him he could see the gleam of pitch in the rough bark, the pine needles hanging from the trees, the scuffed needles on the ground. The forest beyond him, though, fell into an even deeper darkness relative to the light from the lamp. He made his way out of the forest and into a clearing. The sky had cleared and there were stars overhead, a brilliant field of black and stark tiny bits of light. The moon hung just over the hill. He walked for a while through the woods not caring now if he became lost. He headed back toward the top of the hill to the clearing where he had spent the day.

He heard then the yips of coyotes. Normally he would have made sure his tent was zipped up. He didn't have a tent. He listened to them and realized they weren't far away. Instead of walking away from them, he walked toward the sound. He came into a familiar clearing and then at the edge of it, he could see the buck he'd killed. The coyotes were already at the animal. Marshall lowered the gun and fired. He had meant to fire over them, but his bullet hit one of the animals. It snapped back and lay still in the brush. The other coyotes, silver in the moonlight, began to run. Marshall reloaded and fired again and killed another one. He reloaded and waited thinking they would regroup or something and come back together for the meat, but they were gone. He went down to the stag and found that they had hardly eaten any of it. He'd hoped they had eaten enough to make it easier to carry, but they hadn't. The stag was black now in the moonlight where the blood had come out. Marshall strapped the gun to his back and then lowered himself under the heavy intestines of the animal, now sticky with blood. White loops of its intestines had started to slip out. He had the whole thing now up on his back and he just kept taking one step after another down the hill toward the area where he knew the camp was. In the forest he could barely see, but the pine grew far enough apart that the moonlight was there, and finally deep in the night he came out on the road and he slowly, step by step, walked back to the camp.

A car was parked at the campsite. It was a massive Pontiac rusted out and nearly black in the moonlight. The chrome bumpers caught the light, but otherwise there was nothing except for the car. Someone slept in the back of the car. The fire in the pit had guttered low. Marshall dropped the deer near the pit. He found a rope and then threw it over a branch of the fir tree and pulled the deer into the air.

He went down the stream and took off his clothes and then waded out into the middle of the freezing water and washed the smell of the animal off his body. His skin was bright under the dappled shadows. He felt better, and then he grabbed his sleeping bag, and sat down in the grassy patch and before he knew it he was asleep.

He woke with the sun in his face. He heard the voices of the men and the guffaw of a female voice. The sun came through the branches and into his face. He rubbed his eyes and then sat up. He gradually understood that the men sat near the fire. Flames licked up.

"There he is," Keane said. "Back from the dead."

Carnation didn't say anything. He sat in a chair with his belt unbuckled and the buttons on his trouser undone. He held his flask in his lap and didn't even notice Marshall waking up. Marshall went down to the stream and washed his face and then returned to the fire.

The woman sitting at the fire looked at him. She had black hair and a flat nose. She was darkish with faint freckles covering her face, darker on her neck. She wore a man's plaid shirt unbuttoned to the fifth or sixth button. He could see her chest, covered with darker freckles and fine wrinkles. She wore a black bra that pressed her breasts together. The skin on her chest gleamed in patches as if she had spilled butter on herself. She drank a cup of coffee from a tin cup. She smiled at Marshall showing her teeth. She wore lipstick and a bit of the bright red color had nicked a tooth.

Keane handed Marshall a tin cup of coffee. "We thought it best to let you sleep."

"You did it, man," Ernest said. "You brought it back. How did you find it in the dark?"

"I could hear the animals," Marshall said. "I followed them."

"They didn't get much of it. We can cut that off. There'll be plenty of meat for all of us," Keane said. "It's a fine kill. You did a fine job, son."

Carnation made a noise, but then Marshall realized he'd never seen Carnation as drunk as this. He was so drunk that there was no telling if he could even make sense of them. Carnation struggled in the chair and then finally stood. He started to walk directly toward the fire, but then Keane turned him around.

"I'd let him walk into that. Teach the fucker," Ernest said.

"No need to go the hospital today," Keane said. "Let a man check out from the world every now and then if that is what he requires."

Carnation shuffled into the thicket and sent a long, cascading golden spray into the dirt.

"Man, go further from camp if you need to piss," Ernest said.

Carnation returned to his chair. He took a drink and then sat back down and stared at Marshall for several minutes and then turned back to the fire.

"Anyway, Marshall, this is Bernice. Bernice, this is the boy we told you about."

"Nice to meet you, sweetie," she said.

"Hi," Marshall said.

The men had all been with her. Marshall didn't pay attention. The men sat at the campfire that morning as if they were waiting at the barbershop for their hair to be cut, or the dentist for a filling. They killed time doing things they wouldn't normally do because they were waiting instead of doing anything else. Keene was with her. Ernest spent an inordinate amount of time cleaning pots and pans with gravel from the creek and a tiny jar of soap. He rinsed them and dried them off with crumpled sheets of newsprint. Roger moved his camper and spent an inordinate amount of time backing up and driving out to find a perfectly level spot. He then carefully unassembled his Coleman stove and cleaned each part and reassembled it. Occasionally the sound of the woman and Keene—a mumbling, a muffled laugh—drifted from where she had parked. Marshall finally left. He drifted into the bushes as if he was looking for wood. He started to walk through the forest until he was on top of the next ridge. He hoped when he returned that she would be gone. He wanted to learn this particular thing a different way. He didn't want his stepfather loitering around while he learned this thing or his stepfather's buddies around. He dreaded the idea that he would come out of the car after being with her and they would ask him about it. They would of course, wanting to take part in what had happened to him. He didn't have any connection to these men or this woman.

Aileen

Grandmamma knew when each of the houses had been built. The houses in the holler had been built at the time when Old Man Paulsen returned from wandering after the Civil War. He rode the tracks east and north and lived in the forests and wilderness in the years after the war ripped a canyon where there'd been a margin. There was the north and the south and no one knew where the line was between them. Grandmamma said it was like two kissing cousins in love with each other and sick of the other's bad habits. Like any people in love they either had to get married or kill each other. The war ended up resolving the matter in a way that didn't mean they killed each other. It didn't mean they were married either. Force a woman to marry you by raping her, and see how happy that makes your home life. The men in Washington DC and the factories in New England wanted it to be one place, they didn't want it to have two heads, this country, one in Washington and the other in Richmond. So they fought until the South couldn't resist. She had to marry the North or she would die. We will bleed from those wounds for the rest of the life of this country. That's what Grandmamma said about the War. Before the War the Paulsens owned land. When the Emancipation was made it was as good as burning down the farm as cutting the line of Paulsens back to the very beginning. We had people on the Mayflower you know? We go back to the very first families of this country. And when the slaves were freed we lost what we owned. In America, a man is what he owns. Even so, my grandfather said it was a good thing because owning a person is like having dependents who aren't your own. We had put our stock and our futures in men and the men were not to be our stock and our futures. They were to have futures and stock of their own. We lost what was ours without compensation. Just as the people who we owned had lost themselves before this. You might think it was stealing to own a person. When you or I am born, we own ourselves. But when they were born, someone else owned them. I am not saying owning another person is right. I am not saying anything like that at all. There are two views of existence. One is pragmatic because the way of the world has always been intended by God. And we are suffering through the fixed rail of existence. It is ours to endure this life for the rewards of the next. But to struggle is futile and arrogant. The other view is that the world is beyond God's control. He set it in motion and we are to act given this freedom to do what is right or wrong. Our actions are moral. Our family has always subscribed, like the South did, to the first view. The North adhered to the second. Maybe neither is correct. Who knows about this? But in any case, we were a people before and now we are a people after. We began then in a new land above the valleys where we'd started. Old Man Paulsen finally returned to his homeland and was a stranger in them. He wanted to be here and he didn't want to be here and so he climbed into the hills and built the first of our houses. He took a wife from the people already living in the mountains. His sons built the other houses in the valley. And the next generation built the next and the holler was full, and that is how it has been ever since. We lived in the same houses generation after generation since then. The sons of Paulsen grew old in the holler. Three generations read old man Paulsen's sets of Shakespeare, Dickens, the Greeks, and Romans. Their children grew up around the turn of the century. And in turn their children grew up there in the 1920s, losing men in the World War, this being the first war we had fought in since the Civil War. When they returned they wanted to return to life in the holler. They wanted things to be as they Hadbeen; they didn't know that nothing had ever been as it Hadbeen. They didn't know that there was no Hadbeen, that everything had always been changing and to cling to a Hadbeen that never was, was a kind of madness. The holler had been wilderness and then it had been Old Man Paulsen's land.

This was the world according to Grandmamma and for Aileen this told her everything she really needed to know. She yearned to be part of someone else and yet she didn't want to be subsumed by them the way Richmond had been subsumed by Washington. There was something, though, to Richmond and Kentucky and the rest of the South because they had a liberty they wouldn't have if they had won. They knew the terms of their existence. Aileen didn't know if that is how she wanted to be. She could be her own person. She didn't have to live a secret life under or beneath someone else. And yet she felt that is how it was going to be, that a secret life under or beneath someone else was her only option.

In those years of the Great Depression of Grandmamma's middle age and Aileen's childhood the Paulsens were happy and as removed from the world as they had ever been. The growing presence of the outside world in the twenties was too much, a bright light. They were happy to see it burn out. They had their food just as they always had their food.

In the middle of the war, Aileen also found the town to be something other than what it had been growing up. Growing up, the town near Lexington had been nothing at all. A department store during Christmas. A stage where they would see the Shakespeare plays when they were there. She had once seen the HMS Pinafore there as a girl. And the downtown library, a Carnegie Library with lions on the stoop, and Greek columns rising up, was a place to go. She couldn't check out books there but she could walk up the steps and go into the smell of all of those books and she would take them down from the shelf and read them. She even knew how she could sneak around back and get into the books she wasn't supposed to read.

She liked the newspaper math puzzles and games because everything in the world she believed proceeded from simple statements of fact. If she could establish a certainty she knew a law and found solid ground. The entire world operated on certainties, which are axioms, and each one was like a step on the slope of a mountain. Each step may be small but the accumulation of steps brought her to top of the mountain where she could see the forests and valleys and understand the entire world. Only that wasn't possible because the number of steps was limitless and ongoing. She believed a person could understand a small thing. God had worked out the axioms for the entire world and knew when she would do this and that. That was the idea of a fortuneteller. They could understand God's solutions. But that was pure vanity. No one could do that. No one knew what was going to happen and so you had to act because even though it was already going to happen, if you subscribed to one way of looking at the world, it wasn't going to happen unless you acted.

The Paulsen family continued what Grandmamma called The Southern Way. The world was already determined and had routes and patterns and inevitable arcs and it was ours to endure them. We could not change them.

Life in the holler was about to change, they all knew that, but most of the brothers were still in the war. They'd gone early and they would stay late. This is how it always went. Same as any party.

The picnic tables were set up on the knoll over the river. They played horseshoes and ate corn on the cob, watermelon, and chocolate cake. The women and old men who remained drank cold coffee and sat in the shade while the children played. Aileen was old enough now that the boys didn't bother her, but they used to. The ones who really bothered her, her brother Dewey and her cousin Allen, they were in the war now. She remembers Dewey following her through the woods once and she ran up the hill through the leaves that made so much noise and hid behind a rock and he came in there looking for her. "I can hear you like a wild pig," he said. "I'm a pig hunter. I have need for some pork fat." He stood below her. He was just two years older than her and hardly bigger than her but he was a boy and hard from the summer working in the fields and moving things for father. The river was just a distant noise. There was nowhere for her to go under the forest. She should have just kept running because she was a fast runner. They encourage the girls to run in the woods. It was always a girl's fault if a boy caught her. A boy was always supposed to go after a girl. She thought it was similar to how the boys always fought each other. They were always giving each other black eyes. Her brother broke a cousin's collarbone. Her uncle was more angry about the lost work than he was about his son's pain, about the loss of feeling his son still felt in his hands from the broken bone; it was his fault after all for getting into a situation where he was fighting with another boy and if he couldn't take it; if his bones broke, it was his fault. A man needed to take such things and a woman, too, needed to keep everything together. If she didn't have enough sense to stay next to her mother when the boys were around, then she deserved what happened to her if they caught her. Aileen was fast on her feet, but she made a mistake going down to the river to put her feet in and then she saw the boys and so she climbed into the forest. They saw her go. She ran. Now she was on the hillside. Dewey heard her and he came toward her and there was nothing she could do and so she made the best of it. He wasn't mean to her like some of the boys were. They never bruised her or anything, but if she didn't cooperate they would twist her arm. They might not put it in the right place, and then she would bleed for sure.

Her math teacher encouraged Aileen to apply for a scholarship to Kentucky State and she did. She applied and won a math scholarship. It wouldn't cost her anything to go to school. They would, in fact, pay her a little bit of money so she could concentrate on her homework. Her parents, however, were less than pleased by this. "What are you going to with a math scholarship?" they asked. Who will marry a woman who knows calculus?

She was going to wear cardigans and a pleated dress and keep on wearing her horn-rim glasses. She would wear makeup and drink coffee at the coffee shop while she did her math problems. She wanted to work on the problems.

She liked sitting in a classroom at the flat wooden desks where she'd seen the college students listening to their lectures. They kept their books in bags on the floor and worked through the textbook while the professor wrote on the board. The difference between a professor and a teacher was that the professor didn't care if you learned or not. They weren't there to see to it that you learned. They were there to have their knowledge and the student was there to take their knowledge. They didn't want to give it up. She'd seen them holding onto it by making their explanation more obscure and odder as the students pressed them. They would begin to write on the board. They would point out something to some of the people in the classroom. A woman student didn't have to wear makeup. She wore trousers and a blouse. "Why not go all of the way," the professor said. "You are almost there."

"Where is that?" the student asked.

"You are almost a man."

The teacher would never do this but the professor could and didn't care. This is what Aileen wanted from school: no rules and a place where intelligence and knowledge was prized and protected rather than squandered, bullied, beaten down. Her parents thought she did the crossword puzzles in the paper and she didn't. She had liked crossword puzzles, moving up from the local daily to the *New York Times* and then she suddenly became sick of them. She could see how they were written and that she would have to think of new games to make them useful and what was the point of making new games to make them useful when she would just take a piece of pen and paper and make new games that would be of interest to her? She didn't need to harass her father and then the cousin who had followed her into the woods to buy her the *New York Times* from the newsagent in town.

He would come with the newspaper for her to do her

crossword puzzle and now she could say to him that she didn't like crossword puzzles anymore. And she did.

He didn't seem disappointed. He sat with her on the couch and they drank coffee her mother had prepared in the percolator. He lived in a new house at the top of the valley on the other side of the holler. There was a valley, a fork of the river that went down into the plains. They just had a creek up on the holler that made noise in the spring as it carried down the snowmelt from the high country.

The houses of her family occupied good land close to the valley but still in the mountains. It was a steep gravel road to get over the ridge and down into the holler. In the spring, patches of snow, silver and coated with pine needles and the snow having clotted into chucks of ice, still lay in the shadow of the trees. In the summer, she liked to climb up onto the hill and smell the wind as it came down from the cool mountains and into the hot valley. The hot valley sucked up the air and moisture and then sent it off into the mountains where it cooled and dropped rain on the mountainsides and then the cool air rolled down for another round.

What did she want to do at the University?

She didn't want to live in the holler anymore, that's what she wanted to do. She wanted to be someone, somewhere else. She wasn't aware of her thick accent until she was on the streets of Lexington and then she was aware of it. There were soldiers training there. The streets were full of them and they were from all over and they spoke a hundred different ways. They spoke like men from the North. She didn't understand everything they said. She understood the words, just not how they said it.

The girls at school talked about the soldiers. The soldiers were good for a Saturday night out. They bought them gifts. They would take them to the dance hall and afterward buy them dinner. And from the soldiers they learned about the world beyond the mountains. The soldiers, too, didn't know or care about country folk. They were just young men looking for young women. The girls whispered about their presents and laughed.

Her parents thought about the scholarship and then said no. Not only did women from the mountains not go to the city—she would have to live in the city alone—and it was hard enough for the men who'd gone there looking for work. She didn't have to say why. People treated the mountain people differently. Bumpkins.

"But I'll study math. No one has an accent in math."

"A scholarship is like a job. As a job it isn't a well paying one."

"It is job training. It is like they are giving us money. People pay hundreds of dollars for the courses they are giving me." She thought she would appeal to the business sense of her father. He always said, "Don't look a gift horse in the mouth."

"The women in our family have the work they do and they don't do that kind of work," her mother said.

"I am not good at those things."

"You don't need math."

"How do you know what I need?"

"We are your parents."

She turned down the application. She stopped even going to high school. Her father finally sat with her at the kitchen table. He held the tiny coffee cup. The surface was thick with cream and steam. "Why aren't you going to school?"

"What is the use of going to school? I'm a girl."

"You'll finish what you started."

"I started something else," she said. "You finished it for me."

She went back to school. But she also went to Lexington to look for a GI. If she could find a soldier from a far enough place she could go there and she wouldn't have to be a woman who didn't have the chance to learn anything.

She didn't know how, who, what what she was looking for. The first trip she made to Lexington with her girlfriends—they were 17 and 18 years old—they were all nervous. "Do you think we'll meet any soldiers?"

"Do you think they will even notice us?"

They all wore their dancing dresses and knee-high socks and a trace amount of lipstick.

It wasn't that they were chaste. They had a saying among them that a girl would have to be born a pretty fast sprinter to remain a virgin in the hills. They laughed about it not because they thought it was funny, but because like farmers chuckling among themselves about drought or doctors chuckling among themselves about cancer, there was nothing they could do to prevent it except to find it funny and to think about it in terms where they had some kind of control.

"Do you think you'll find an interested man?"

"Oh yes."

"I wonder if anyone will look at me twice."

"Oh yes."

"I wonder if I find out if they are interesting at all between their panting and groaning. That is what men do: pant and groan. Since that's all they do, you can't find out anything that you need to know about them."

They went to the enlisted dance hall looking for officers. The woman at the door checked their coats and purses. She asked them where they were from and Aileen said "Beechmont," in her phoniest voice possible and this got them. The woman laughed and didn't ask them any more questions. Just through an answer to a question, they might give it away. It might be very clear where they were from and if she knew they were from the mountains, she would never let them in, they thought.

Aileen wondered, though, because she let them into the dance hall anyway so maybe she thought they were lying about Beechmont and meant somewhere else. That was the idea Aileen had—to tell a kind of lie that someone else would tell.

This was an Odd Fellows hall several stories tall with a balcony where the band played. From the floor they could just see the musicians, a colored band, that struck Aileen as exotic. The floor was full of Army men in their Class A's. Most of the men had taken off their jackets and danced not in the sedate waltz and shuffle that Aileen was used to from the holler but in a way she couldn't even fathom. She wasn't shy about dancing. She knew she wasn't a beauty either, and this still didn't make her shy about dancing, rather she didn't know what to do with her body, exactly. Her friends had been in these dances before and she followed them out to the floor and tried to learn the dances. She'd played around with jazz steps, the Lindy and even before that the Charleston—an old-fashioned joke dance they would do sometimes. But what was happening here was beyond her, everyone swayed and moved, men lost their footing on the shiny floor and didn't fall but skidded and shuffled and this was part of the dance, too. Girls hiked up the skirts so they could move their legs. They threw them up when they got the chance, showing their underwear. Aileen danced, careful to follow the more sedate patterns, and after a while went to the wall.

It was at the wall that she ran into Orton for the first time. He was stalking the wall for shy girls and she knew that is what he was doing because he'd just been talking to a girl who was so shy she wouldn't even talk to him. He wore his jacket—which meant to Aileen that he wasn't dancing—and this was fine with her because she didn't know what to do and the place being strange and full of officers she didn't want to do something she shouldn't have done, something that would give her away as having come from the mountains, some slip of her accent—she noticed he wore his jacket because it had medals on it and his rank, a captain, conspicuously displayed.

He nodded his head and she realized, because she'd been out on the floor moving, that he wasn't going to talk to her, she had shown signs of life. Is that how it was? He was busy looking for the frightened birds on the sides of the dance floor like a lizard. That's what she thought about him then, dressed in green on the margins of the dance hall, that he was a fence lizard.

Her feeling that she had something over on him, this feeling, forced her to pull him from the side of the wall and out onto the floor. "Wait a minute," he said.

"You can wait in a minute," she said.

She started to keep the moves aligned to what she thought people were doing around her and then she realized as she tried to copy what they were doing that they were all copying each other, no one here really knew the moves if there were even moves. It was all more of a feeling than anything else, a feeling they captured by making their bodies move and so she was making her body move and he was making his body move because he wanted to keep his suave exterior, his captain's rank, in a club where just about all of the men were enlisted.

They danced and she wouldn't stop because she wanted to wear him out.

And finally exhausted they struggled to the side of the hall like struggling to shore. She'd lost her friends. She looked around, realized the hall was clearing out.

Orton was looking at her and he shook his head. And she could see from his looking at her that he didn't know what to think about her. He had for one thing the wrong idea about her. She knew that much about what he was thinking about her. He thought she was a wild woman and that she had somehow picked him. And this knowing what he thought about her before he even said anything and knowing that this thing that he thought about her was not correct made her feel even more like she had something over on him and that having something over on him made her feel even safer, more in control, than she had felt in the entire time she was growing up.

"I like dancing," she said.

"Dancing is swell," he said. She could hear in his voice that this was not something he would say and he was trying on a personae, too; he didn't have a clear bead on what he was trying on and so he said things that sounded like the personae rather than just the person he wanted to be and then spoke from that person.

She found her coat. "I have to be going," she said.

"I'll buy a coffee?"

"Yes," she said.

They went out into the street and it was full of pairs of soldiers and women like her. Hundreds of pairs. He led her through this crowd, not holding her hand the way she would have liked, so she took his hand and said slow down.

And then they were holding hands but he still moved through the crowd quickly and she hustled beside him until they came onto an empty street. There were a few closed storefronts and then there was a bakery.

"What would you like?"

"Coffee and some bread and butter."

"They have pie. They have really good pie here."

"I want what I want," she said. She listened to herself talk and felt this was how she wanted to be, but she didn't know it then, that she'd somehow become entangled with this somewhat short, stocky man wearing the rank of captain.

He ordered coffee and a slice of German chocolate cake.

They sat at the counter looking out into the street that was pretty much empty now.

"So where are you from?" he asked her.

"From Kentucky," she said.

"Lexington?"

"No. A little place you probably never heard of."

"Where?"

"Out there," she said. "How about you?"

He told her about Iowa, where he grew up on a farm.

"I grew up on a farm, too," she said. "My father owns the farm. Everyone else has moved on to do something else, and my brothers do not want to be farmers. My family has lived out there forever."

"My family will have that farm for as long as there is my family," Orton said. "I don't go there much anymore, though. Got kicked out over some trouble when I was fourteen."

This didn't strike Aileen odd at the time. Later, it would strike her as odd, but at the time in the 1930s, fourteen seemed plenty old for a person to act up and then have to suffer the consequences. It just meant the person was headstrong. And she could see just from looking at him that he was headstrong. He was still a child, though.

"I wandered around some after that. Saw a lot of things and ended up in this place on the West Coast and found work in the shipyard and then at an airplane company. Thought I had it made when the war broke out. Plenty of work, plenty of money, and then I was inducted and sent off."

"Where did you got to college?"

"College—"

He wasn't an officer. She had this over him as well.

They talked for a while longer and then she said,

"When can I talk to you again. How do I get in contact with you?"

She gave him her address. He wanted her phone number. "I can't give that to you," she said.

"How about next weekend. We can meet in the lobby of the Savoy and go do something. I'll take you out for something to eat?"

"See you next weekend, private."

She didn't turn around and see what he said; she just went back to the bus stop. The other girls were there and they inspected each other to make sure they didn't look too disheveled and they were on their way home.

A letter was in the box two days later. He wrote how pleased he was to find someone he could talk to. She wasn't sure about that. He wrote, too, about the mistake of his rank. He had lost his jacket. Or it was stolen. He didn't know which. So he borrowed his friend's. A private with a friend who was an officer.

His name on the return address was the name on the jacket.

So she had this over him as well. He was a bad liar.

It wasn't entirely that she had something over on him. He had made her surprise herself with her urbane-ness and her ability to go along with her image of herself. She'd been in the city until late with a man and she held her own with him—she had something over on him— she loved sitting at the bakery counter looking past the chrome and plate glass at the street and the occasional person passing by. She loved coming out of the dance hall still flushed and hot into the cool city air with the sound of buses and cars and the crowd of GIs and girls. And he himself had talked to her, not like the high school boys who only saw her from her family as a future mother,

which she was, but right now she was something else—
she was just like any man and she was entitled to have
some fun and if her family wouldn't let her go to college,
they couldn't stop her escaping them to do something else
she wanted to do.

That week she felt wistfulness. She played in the forest
above the house turning the stumps of the virgin trees
into castles, houses, and island. She'd walk down the
road to the highway were the mailbox lay between two
tall posts her father had hammered into the ground after
thugs battered down the old tin box. Everything in the
valley had a story and would always be here, she figured.
There wasn't any room for her in this place. It was her
family's place.

She met Orton in the lobby of the Savoy. He wore his real
Class-A's this time. "It turned up," he said.

"Pardon?" She said.

"The jacket."

"Do you like British food?"

"Don't they eat the same thing as everyone else?" She
hadn't heard of an English restaurant before and she
thought about Dickens and it never struck her that they
had different food in those books. Not like the German
or French books she'd read. She always thought it was a
French restaurant you were supposed to go to be fancy,
but then she realized he was trying to be worldly—or that
he really was and he thought she might like it.

"Pie or bread and you choose bread," he said.

"Yes."

"So given the cuisine of the world, I think you'd like
English. Besides it is good to eat."

The place had a sandwich board outside and was in a
Tudor mansion. They went inside and it had candles on

the table and they drank tea before their food arrived. They ate shepherds pie and she liked it a lot. They drank more tea and then, jittery and warm, they walked down the street.

She didn't know where they were going.

They ended up back at the Savoy.

"Would you like to come up and have a drink?"

"You're staying here?"

"Just for the weekend," he said.

"I don't drink, really."

"All the better," he said.

"I don't know."

"I've got a loaf of bread."

She could go up if she wanted. Everything proceeded at this point as she had wanted it.

She went up with him and his room had a view of the city. There was a table with a bottle of red wine and two glasses.

He had a loaf of bread and some cheese.

She ate a slice of the bread and cheese and he poured the wine.

The wine tasted bitter to her but she could also taste that it was good. There wasn't much in the glass and then after drinking about half of it she felt warm and flushed and a little excited. She wanted to jump up and do something. Dance? She wouldn't dance here.

Orton had taken his jacket off. He drank his glass.

He refilled her glass and poured himself his glass and then picked it up and sat on the bed to look out the window. She took her glass and sat on the windowsill and looked out as well.

She realized then that she was in a room with a boy and a bed and knew what he wanted to do and she didn't want to do this but then he would try force her to do it.

She should just go. She could just grab her things and

go and then she would be out of the room, but she was having a good time feeling the wine in her and Orton was asking about Kentucky and she liked talking about Kentucky and so she told him about Kentucky. She thought again about grabbing her things. They talked for a long time. They drank all of the wine. It was time for her to get back to the bus.

"I can drive you."

"How can you drive me?"

"I have a car."

"I don't know if it will be more rapid."

"Let me drive you."

"You can't drive me all of the way home."

"Most of the way," he said.

And with that he decided to rape her or rather he had sex with her or rather she did not want to have sex with him right then and understood that because she had not left when she had the chance, that she had said yes even if she cried and asked him not to, why did he want to do this now and wreck everything? That is what she didn't understand. Why did he go and do this now and she would never have something over on him even if it was something silly like dressing up in a uniform that was not his—she did not want to have sex with him but she understood what had to be done and she let the things that had to be done. And then he kissed her and said she was good at this. He was pleased she had protested, she could tell about that. The worst thing she could have done was to like it and how could any woman like it? It remained for her the furthest thing from her mind that this act had anything to do with childbirth or conception and even further that there were women anywhere who really liked it. This act was to her a compulsive male act, this discharge from the penis like pissing on her. Was he pissing on her? It was a different kind of piss, more like puss.

On the drive back, Orton told her he was shipping out on Wednesday.

"Where are you going?"

"Greenland," he said.

"Where is Greenland?" She had heard of it, but it was one of those places she never thought much about.

"It is the first place in North America where Europeans landed. The Vikings tried to live there, but it was too cold for the Vikings and they died. Only the Eskimos have survived in Greenland."

"How does an Eskimo survive where Vikings can't?"

"They don't eat grains, Eskimos. They survive on seal fat and fish. No sugar even. When the first people met the Eskimos, they were pure: They were as we are supposed to be. That is how they survived in Greenland."

She had never been on the road from Lexington to her house in a car before. They passed the bus just outside of Lexington and he asked if she would like to stop and get a coffee before he dropped her off in her town.

"No thank you," she said.

"I'll write to you," he said.

She didn't expect that he would. And she was glad to put Orton out of her mind.

He wrote to her from Greenland. Long, beautifully written letters about living in the cold. The letters were almost as if they were from someone else. She felt no connection to Orton, the short, stocky man she'd known in Lexington. Rather she felt they were this postmark address and she looked forward to the letters as he tried to unravel the mysteries of Greenland. The European War began to draw to a close and the Pacific War was won but had to be finished and no one looked forward to the finishing of the war because there would be a lot of bloodshed all around. Orton included photographs of the Quonset hut where he lived. He spent his days writing these letters and reading the books he meant to read. "Except for missing you," he said. "This is the best place and time I've ever lived."

She was somehow pregnant. She missed her period two weeks after Orton was gone and she didn't think about it because what is there to miss? And then the next month it was gone, too, and she was worried she was sick. She'd heard of women so sick they didn't menstruate anymore. Was she one of them? What did she have? And then the third month she realized she was pregnant. She didn't know how she'd become pregnant. She knew it had something to with loving a boy. She'd been in love with Orton for a week. Was that all it took?

When she told her mother she knew she would be in trouble but she also knew that the family would be able to deal with it; women in the holler had children like this all of the time. It was not disgraceful but rather an indication of their fertility, their ability, their attractiveness. They kept the women who came down like this in the valley, though, because in town, unwed mothers were not welcome. It was more common now with the war, these mothers. People wouldn't slight her, but they wouldn't be real nice to her either. She wasn't pretty enough for them to be nice to her. They'd think someone had taken advantage of her somehow. How was this any different from just being a girl in the valley? Aileen didn't know. But it was.

She also let Orton know, since she figured he was the father. She figured she would never hear from him again after that letter. She was sort of grateful to be rid of him although she'd miss his writing about Greenland. She had the old letters in any case.

And then he sent her a telegram. WONDERFUL! WHEN I RETURN WE WILL MARRY.

And then after that a dozen-page letter arrived explaining his happiness, his hopes, and long plans for their marriage and life together. She had never read anything so terrible.

Her family skeptically regarded this development. We will see if this young man who we have never met returns from the end of the war. We have seen this situation before and will see it again. We will see.

She had this promise then while he was gone, this promise that he would return. She was not the only woman in the valley to get pregnant. And many of the girls didn't know when the fathers would return. It wasn't so much a source of shame among the people in the valley as a kind of response to what was happening; unexpected things happened and the visiting Army had left their children behind as they always did. They would make these babies country people just like they were country people. They weren't country people before they came to the valleys. The country had made them country people.

The women expecting children without fathers all became regular churchgoers and on Sunday afternoon they would sit in the shade of the churchyard while everyone ate the afternoon potluck. They brought gelatin ambrosia, corn on the cob, fresh baked rolls, meatloaf festooned with bacon and hunks of canned pineapple drained of the fluid. There were platters of cookies and always a cake. The women cultivated finicky eating habits as a sign of their pregnancy and because the group of them were comprised of everyone from the owner of the grocer's daughter down to Ed Hinky's child. Ed Hinky hadn't worked a day in his life and managed to find a house and a beautiful wife. He was poor but they got by on his gathering roots from the forest and doing odd jobs. He drank but not often and when he did everyone in the valley knew to watch him and make sure he didn't pass out somewhere where he might die of exposure.

The letters from Orton kept coming and the war kept going and during that summer as her stomach grew and she settled into life in the valley, not as a university student or as a young woman looking for a family. Less was expected of her because of her condition and so she read and studied in secret to go to the university once Orton came to take her away from the holler. She wasn't sure if that is how it would work. Why not, though, why couldn't she go to night school or something while he watched the baby? It wasn't too much to hope for.

The war with Japan ended suddenly. Everyone was poised for the final long battle and like a relief it ended. The troops were going to be home and before she knew it she was eight months pregnant and about to give birth and Orton did come back. He came to the house and shook her father's hand. He wore his Class A's. He was a sergeant now. "Are you really?"

"Yes, I am."

He wore his Class A's and he talked to her father and her father was proud to have him in their house. Her father said this to Orton. For her father to say anything like this to anyone's face meant he really was proud because he didn't want anyone getting a big head. In his estimation the worst thing that anyone could do to anyone else was to give them a big head.

Orton smiled and after dinner her father and Orton sat out on the porch and drank whiskey until they were both squinting and sweating and laughing in whispers. Although Aileen didn't abide by drinking, just as her mother didn't, it was a special occasion. And if he was going to have the occasional drink and get drunk like her father—whisky was a good test as she understood it, which was why her father probably got him drunk to test out what kind of drunk he was—and as she was going to bed she heard her father say something like "What are you doing here where you don't belong with my daughter?" She stopped on the stairs and realized how she didn't know this man, Orton. She knew her father and watched him as he tried to get a three-hour understanding of Orton. Orton stepped back and walked half-way down the stairs, his hands over his head and he turned to look at her father and he said, "I'm sorry. I'm sorry."

"What do you mean?" her father asked.

"I'm sorry," he said again.

"You are drunk son."

She didn't know what her father had learned from the exchange but she figured he'd tell her.

Orton stayed at the house, writing letters. She wasn't sure to whom. "I got in the habit of writing things down," he told her. "So I write them down. They are kind of like letters to myself, I guess. I could think of them that way. I write my letters to myself."

She liked this, that he was someone who did something like this. Orton did little else during that week he was there and then he went on a hunting trip into the mountains with one of her brothers and that was when her father talked to her about Orton.

"He came back for you and his child, so there isn't much I can do about it now."

"You can do something."

"He's here now. He's a right to you. I didn't think I'd wish this on my grandchild, that it'd be a bastard, but spending some time with that man has made me think that."

Aileen didn't know what to do.

"He's cowardly and I think he might be lazy and a showoff."

"He has some good qualities."

"To a nineteen-year-old girl I think he might have some good qualities."

She became angry then that her father was damning her to him and also dismissing him. He was dismissing her and his grandchild. Didn't he care?

"Then do something about it. I realize I've made a mistake."

"Your choice was made a long time ago," he said.

She had never made a choice. She didn't know what had happened to her. She had loved him for two days, or she had a crush on him, but she didn't know him then, she had an idea of him, but not anything about him that she really knew. She didn't know anything about him when she had loved him and became pregnant. She would never love anyone again. She would not love him again because she didn't want to have any more children.

When Orton came back from his trip, Aileen's father suggested that he might want to take Aileen to visit his folks and get married before the baby was born.

In private Orton asked Aileen about her father. "Does he like me?"

"I am his little girl," she said.

"You are my little girl now," he said.

"So how would you like someone who took me away from you?"

"No one is taking me away from you."

"You are taking me away from my father. You have not treated me as a gentleman should treat a woman who he would have as his wife."

"I am a lucky man," Orton said. "How could your father like a man as lucky as me?"

They packed their bags and took a train to St. Louis.

She was too pregnant to travel but he persuaded them to let her travel. She was too pregnant even if they let her. The jostling of the train and the size of the baby inside her made for a painful trip.

They went to a hotel in St. Louis.

She wasn't sure at that point. Should they get married? She didn't know him and he didn't know her. They knew each other as pen pals; she liked his letters but here he was in the morning, wearing his t-shirt and slacks and drinking the instant coffee at the hotel. They sat at the little table and drank coffee before they went out for breakfast. He had his hard stubble. He smiled to reveal all of his teeth. The skin around his eyes pinched into a deep fold.

"You don't want to get married to me?" he asked.

"Are you asking me to marry you?" she asked.

"I am."

She lifted out her hand and he fumbled around the room. "She wants a ring," he said to himself.

She held her hand up and started to cry and he found a paper straw and slipped that around her finger and tied a not. "A note for a ring," he said.

She smiled at him and thought how this could be a moment. If he'd just done it right. If he'd already had the piece of paper with the knot tied, if he'd managed to slip it onto her finger to get it sized correctly, then he could have slipped it onto her. It would have been all right, but now it wasn't right.

She thought she could change the story in her head. She could make it right. She had something over on him still. He proposed to her without a ring. Was there a bigger thing than that to have over on someone who might be your husband? Might be? The matter was as good as settled. There was nothing she could do about it.

"Yes," she said. She was crying and believed he would be fooled into thinking her crying was because she was happy. How could she be happy when the man who proposed to her didn't have a ring and she was eight months pregnant? But she could not think about those things. She could not play out the story of the wrongs done to her because they were too long and she told herself she wouldn't do that anymore. That part of her new life wasn't to catalog the moments of offense and then shuffle through them.

Once she retold herself the story it was all right and they dressed in their church clothes. She wore a long, dark blue skirt that still fit. He wore his black suit with the handkerchief in the pocket. They went to breakfast. She wasn't feeling well by the time they sat down. She could smell from the table , bacon, fried eggs, and sputtering pots of grease. She asked for a fruit plate and when the melon and strawberries arrived she sprinkled salt on them.

"What are you doing?"

"I crave salt," she said. "I crave savory."

"But this is a restaurant," he said.

"You're sitting with a woman in a place like this who is eight months pregnant and neither of us has a ring on our fingers."

"We'll get rings."

"I want a diamond," she said. She said this because she knew he wouldn't be able to produce one or if he did it would come at a great expense to him. She wanted to see if he would do it.

He asked for the check and paid. She checked the tip and saw that he hadn't left any.

"Why aren't you tipping?"

"I'm saving up for your diamond ring," he said.

"You think it is unreasonable for me to ask for a diamond ring?"

"We are a young family just starting out."

"You are the one who made me this way," she said.

"You are the one who did this to me."

"We both did it," he said.

What, she wondered, had she done to do this?

He went to a department store with her. They endured the gaze of the woman at the counter to choose rings. They had them fitted and then he asked her to pick out a diamond ring.

"You are supposed to pick it," she said.

He picked out the smallest, puniest diamond they had. A speck on a silver ring.

The woman at the counter glanced at Aileen. She smiled and said, "That's a wonderful ring. It is the one I would have picked out myself."

Aileen was pleased she said this because even if it was a lie it was a convincing lie and even if it was a convincing lie this ring gave her something on Orton and she was beginning to think she needed something on Orton.

They took their rings and she felt better about it. He was happy too and hugged her on the street and they went to the courthouse and applied for a license. The desk they waited at was a large wooden hulk battered and worn from the traffic of people getting marriage licenses. The hallway was full of couples like themselves, trim young men with military haircuts and women, not all of them unblemished by contact with their husbands.

This made Aileen feel much better. Her story wasn't the only one like this.

They had the certificate and took a cab to the edge of town and talked about their future together about baby names about what things would be like and where they would go and they didn't know where they would go they could go anywhere they had no idea where they would go and so they would go there wherever that was.

The justice of the peace married them the next day. As a honeymoon, they took the train to Cedar Rapids. He did book a private car, but this was more for his own reasons than to make the trip memorable.

None of his family came to greet him at the station. "Do they know you are coming?"

"I called ahead," he said. "But my family and I had a falling out when I was young."

"Are they going to hate me?"

"I don't know. They will like you because my marriage to you will settle some things for them. They will understand I'm grown up and the things they are mad at me about are just the things a person gets mad at a child about. It makes no sense to keep being angry at me."

The house sat on a long ascending bump rising from the surrounding fields with no discernible difference in elevation. Once they were near the house they could see the countryside for miles. Countryside was hyperbole. A parking lot had more character. The country was just fields with occasional rows of poplars to break the wind. The new barn was painted white and roofed with conglomerate shingles. Orton said it looked more like a factory then a barn. The only hint, aside from the practical indications of the vents, was the weather vane on top of the roof, a cow pointed to the northeast. The old barn lay on the other side of the house down the slope with the creek. The pond was edged with cattails and a weeping willow. "It's as it was and not as it was," Orton said. "It is all different now and not at all as I remember it." The cab parked and Orton took everything out of the trunk and paid the man. The cab drove away and left Aileen then on the dusty flat ground made even more flat by the mound the house stood on, by the absolute vertical rise of the windbreak poplars, by the unremittingly level horizon. She'd grown up in the hills without any sense of the world around her. There was always a mountain slope in front of her and behind her. There was always something blocking her view of the rest of the world. Here, she could get a sense of it all, but there was nothing of which to get a sense.

Orton's mother ran the farm. There was no sign of Orton's father and no one said anything about there ever being a father. Orton was the only boy in the family. He had three sisters and the mother and they all lived in the farm and they lived there like men. His mother was driving the tractor cutting grass when the cab dropped them off. "She's out in the fields," Orton's sister said. She stood in the front foyer wearing overalls with a ratty cardigan over them. She wasn't wearing shoes and asked them to take their shoes off if they were going to come into the house. "Those are her rules."

She didn't say who she was and so Aileen had to guess who she was and she slowly began to realize that she was Orton's mother. The sister smiled. "We heard you were married," she said to Aileen. "Just last week."

"Yes."

"None too soon," she said.

Aileen tried to remember the names of the sisters. She couldn't remember them, not because Orton hadn't told her but because the way he told her was like this was trivia from his life; he had been in a middle school with the name of a president. She didn't remember the name of the president. He'd lived for a time in a city on the West Coast, she didn't remember which city except that it was one she'd heard of and that she still didn't know anything about it. She'd been told the names of the sisters but she didn't know their names or dispositions and his sister took them into the kitchen and sat them down at the table. "Coffee?"

Aileen would have liked coffee but she was afraid of drinking the coffee and of her stomach because her stomach was acidic. "Do you have cream?" she asked.

"Do we have cream? My dear, this is a farm," she said.

The sister looked at Orton—a pointed suggestion of raised eyebrows. It figured she was a stupid one because she'd allowed him to marry her. This was for both of their benefits. This was Orton's place and her place was down with Orton.

"You've been away a long time, Orton."

"When is mother going to come in from the field?"

"We all have our work to finish today, Orton, before we drop everything to see you. You left the way you did. Normally, a young man who leaves like that doesn't come back. You came back after all of that."

"I was fourteen."

"All the worse. What do you think is here for you?"

"I wanted to come home."

"Laynie isn't here, you know. She only comes to work on the farm in the busy season."

"If it isn't the busy season then why isn't Mother here?"

"She still has her things to finish before she can sit down even to just sit down with you."

They sat in the kitchen and drank their coffee.

"It is good to see you. You look different and the same, you know. I can see that it is you."

"Have you read my letters?"

"Your letters aren't you. They are another you."

"It's my name on the letters."

"You wrote the letters but you wrote them to do what you needed the letters to do and now you are here and you can't hide. You have to show the whole truth, now. You seem different but I know you well enough to know that is probably not true."

"When I left, I was fourteen."

That doesn't change anything. We are who we are no matter what age we were." She examined Aileen. "When are you due?"

"I am ready to have my baby any day. I could've had my baby on the train or the hotel room in St. Louis."

"Orton?" she asked. "Should we get a doctor?"

"We shouldn't get a doctor," he said. "She's been like this for weeks."

They sat in the kitchen for a long time not saying anything. They drank their coffee and placed the cups on the kitchen table. They looked outside at the flat horizon, the line of trees in the distance that moved a little, and moved, all of them, every time Aileen shuffled, which she had to sitting on the hard wooden Sears and Roebuck kitchen chair.

"I need to use the powder room," Aileen said.

"Come on, dear," she finally said. She led Aileen down a hallway. She thought at first that the *dear* was like crossing a threshold, but the woman kept her dour expression. She could not be bothered and she was being bothered. She had things she had to do and while she did things like this with her, she was not doing the things she had to be doing. She opened the door to the bathroom. It was clearly an addition to the house, a rickety structure slightly separate from the entire house. Cold air came through the seams in the wall where it had been attached to the house. She sat on the toilet and then looked up at the cobwebs in the ceiling and slowly her unsettled stomach began to settle down. After she'd peed she sat in the silence. She didn't want to come out.

The sister knocked on the door. "Aileen? Are you well?"

"I am not in labor. I just need some time."

"Would you like to lie yourself down?"

"I would like to rest for a spell."

"We have a room for you two to stay. To stay for a bit."

Aileen was tired and sitting down and sleeping would be a good situation. She could sit down and sleep for a long time. That would be just the thing. She could sit down for a long time and until she felt better that would be just right. She opened the door and followed Orton's sister up the stairs. From the second story the windows looked out over everything in view. They were open. There wasn't any artificial light upstairs and there didn't need to be; they could see over everything. The sister opened a room for her to lay down in. The room had a large wooden bed. The bed was buried under quilts. A whitewashed chest of drawers sat against one wall with a basin and pitcher full of water. "You may lay here for some time, and come downstairs when you feel well. We will hear you walking when you wake so no need to call it."

Aileen lay on the bed. It was firm. She removed her shoes. She loosened her skirt, and removed her brassier. Her breasts hurt after the long train ride, after they began to swell because of her situation. She kept her blouse on though. She rested in the bed and the sheets were clean and smelled like the wind and grasses where it air-dried. What would she do? She was going to have this baby any minute.

The house creaked in the wind. The shadows came from the window and arced across the ceiling. She thought she saw them move but then was aware that she was falling asleep and waking and they were moving but they were moving as slowly as she was moving and then she woke and Orton was in bed with her. It was dark outside. She was thirsty. The suitcases were in the room. She removed her clothes and put on her dressing gown and walked down the hallway. She could hear the sound of movement in the dark house then a clack and creak and each step sounded like she was splintering the floorboards. The house had a kind of yeasty smell, a house where things were baked and cooked and washed. She felt like she could not stay in a house like this because in the house where she grew up these things were the last things that anyone did, first they did the reading they had to do and then after the reading they had to do they worked on the school work they had to work on if there was time left in the day—provided they didn't go swimming they went swimming. In this house, though, everything seemed clean in a way that would almost require constant diligence. She could not tell if this is what had been applied.

In the kitchen there was a plate with a note with her name on it. It said. "If you come into the kitchen when you wake, here is some dinner for you and your baby. Welcome. Milk is in the refrigerator."

She wanted milk. She opened the refrigerator and took out the jug of milk, a clay urn she could barely pick up and poured it into a glass. The milk came out mixed with yellow globs of cream and filled the glass almost to the top. She drank the glass and ate the dinner, a roast beef sandwich. There was a piece of pie, too. She ate this and felt full. Too full. She went to the cool room where the toilet was and peed. She went back to the kitchen to wash her hands. The light over the prairie came from the moon and she could see the same features. The light was less and changed the entire aspect of the land, but not that much. She realized. What roughness there was—the silhouette of the poplars, the willow—would become imprinted in her memory like tines of a key.

An old woman stood at the top of the stairs. "What are you doing in my house?" she asked.

"My name is Aileen."

"I know what you are."

"I'm Orton's wife."

The woman stood at the top of the stairs for a long time. Aileen waited for her to say a word. Aileen could hear the house in the dark. It made tiny noises as the wood settled, as water trickled from the gutters. It was mostly a silent house, but Aileen didn't know what to make of the sounds and the woman just standing at the top of the stairs. The old woman at last said, "I expect you'll have the child any day now."

"Yes. Any day now."

"It looks like a girl to me," she said.

"Fifty-fifty chance," Aileen said.

"It's already determined," the woman said. "We sleep in our beds in this house."

"I went to sleep early because of the trip. I had to eat."

The woman grumbled something Aileen couldn't hear and she began to make her way back up the stairs. "Nice to meet you," Aileen called.

The noise from downstairs woke them. It was still dark outside. "What time is it?"

"Why?"

"I thought you grew up on a farm."

"I did, the women didn't wake up until dawn and the men—if they had to wake up before dawn—didn't make a racket."

"The racket is helping them wake up," he said. He laughed when he said it.

Later when the sun finally came into their room, Aileen said to Orton. "I don't think your family likes me."

"You don't have anything to do with it. It's me that they don't like."

"Why did we return here?"

"This is home. I had planned to come back here after the war. I didn't know that you'd happen during the war."

"We could have gone anywhere."

"I need to find employment."

"What about your military money?"

"We need that money. I don't want to just spend it on trying to get on. I need a job. I had work before the war. They'll give me something."

"This house is so cold."

"Bundle up," he said.

"I don't like it here."

"We won't be here long," he said.

The house was empty when they went downstairs. Orton fixed her breakfast, porridge with molasses and slices of toast and a glass of milk with a little coffee in it. He washed the dishes when he finished and put them away.

He spent the morning writing letters to his old bosses and then he said he was going to town to mail them. "Do you want to come along?"

"I will wait upstairs and read," she said. She climbed up the stairs and lay on the bed and looked outside at the cumulous clouds sweeping across the sky, at the fields with their long grasses turning in the wind. She read her book and waited. She could feel the baby moving slightly in her stomach and she wondered if when she finally did give birth if that would be it, that the sisters would turn around. She started to go into labor. She held the bedpost until the contraction subsided. She got ready to go to the hospital. She had another contraction and then she was in labor.

Everyone was outside working.

She struggled through the afternoon and then at dusk Orton came up the stairs with food for her and he saw her.

"You are having the baby?"

"Yes," she said.

He took her down the stairs and drove in his sister's truck to the hospital. On the way in her water broke.

"I expect I'll have to wash that out before I return sister's truck," Orton said.

She had a baby girl. And in the weeks after the birth she

was busy with the child. Orton left a week after the baby was born for Seattle where the company he'd worked at before the war rehired him. He went to work out the arrangements.

The sisters moved her into a downstairs room and looked after her.

They said to her, "Maybe this will change Orton. He seems much older. He seems to possess a sense of responsibility. He didn't used to be like that," they said.

"What did he used to be like?" She wanted to ask what had he done? What could a fourteen-year-old boy have done?

"It does not matter what he used to be like," the sister said. "He can't be like that any longer."

When Orton returned from the Pacific Northwest he returned with a new diamond ring for Aileen. She was pleased and showed the sisters and she realized as she showed them the ring that her ring was for them. She missed her old ring. Her old ring gave her something over him and now she had nothing over him. He had done the best he could, the story would go, and when he was flush, he had spent the money on her. He had a home for her to move to, a job working in the factory not three miles from the place. "I could walk," he said, but there was no need. He drove a new car and a week after he returned. They set out across the country with the baby sleeping in her arms.

Mary

On the way to the bus in the spring, Mary stopped at the field that bordered the lot of forest her father owned and the dairy farm just up the hill. The dairy farm had long fields that sloped up to the small hill. The small hill had older trees on it, fir with naked, broken snags of heads. In the field several horses slowly edged over to her. They snorted, sending up plumes of white breath. Their hooves churned up the muck in the field. They didn't have enough room in the field and the entire field was just black, churned mud. The fence here was old and the barbwire had started to rust. The muddy ditch was full of cattails and bracken fern and a clear trickle of running rainwater, but it was just wide enough that she couldn't lean across the ditch. She would plunge into the ditch and get mud up to her calves. She stood on the gravel shoulder and picked long strands of grass and threw them toward the horses. They leaned forward but the grass just floated away in the movement of air over the field. It wasn't really wind because a wind would have cleared the thick smog clinging to the ground.

Marshall rode his bike to school, leaving hours before anyone else woke. He rose early because he liked to go to the coffee shop near the High School and work on his math homework. Mary woke when she first heard her brother closing the door to the shed outside with its screechy hinges and then she could hear the rattling clack of the used Schwinn he'd bought at the junk yard in Maple Valley and had repaired himself, using a manual he checked out from the library. Passing on the road near them she was aware of how alone she was right then in the world with those horses that wanted to get the grass she had to offer them and couldn't. She could hear the plop and suck of their hooves in the mud. She could hear the warp and clatter of the tin line in the long wire fence. And the air moved through her in cold gusts. Beyond the sphere of what she could see, the entire universe dropped away. She had fifteen minutes to get to the edge of the road and then climb the embankment to the bus stop on the highway where the children from the farms lined up. She might pass a couple of them who would climb down the embankment to the old farm road to smoke while they waited for the bus. It only got worse there. They never looked at her because they weren't exactly sure who she was. She never said, "Hi," to them, and when they did ask her who she was, she had told them she was a foreign exchange student living with a family in the woods beyond the dairy field. "Oh yeah, where are you from?" "Belgium," Mary said. "What's Belgium like?" She said, "I can't speak English." And they said, "How do you expect to learn to speak American if you don't talk with us?" "I don't know what you mean," she said. She didn't care if they thought it was a lie. Now they just looked at her. They never spoke to her.

At school the bright light in the hallway ceiling bothered her. She hurried to her homeroom, took off her coat and draped it over the back of her chair and then took out her notebook and recorded facts about the horses.

Her sister left the house just as Mary left the house. Her boyfriend, who worked in a downtown design firm as a typesetter, picked her up in his bright red T-bird with just room for the two of them and he dropped her off at school. He lived in a house in Kent with his mother. Mary had been there once after church. Clark's mother was still at her church. Margaret and Clark closed the door to the basement leaving Mary to wander through the house. They had a field behind their house, too, but the grass had turned wild and blackberries had started to creep in. The yard to their house was very neatly mowed. Their orchard, three rows of eight trees—although the last row had one stump and only seven trees—had white painted trunks. White sheets flapped from the clothesline behind the house. The house itself sat on a tall foundation and light came in from the field. The kitchen had glass shelves with glass bottles on them. Not even a speck of dust had been allowed to cling to the glass. The light came through and made the entire collection glow and sparkle.

Clark came up the stairs wearing his Sunday suit again and combing his hair. "Oh hi, Mary."

"MMM," Mary said.

"Would you like a soda? We've got a Coca-Cola somewhere."

"No thank you," she said.

He sat down on the living room couch. Mary thought there was something nice about their living room and then she realized that they didn't have a TV console. They had a phonograph machine, a really old one, against one wall. They had a single bookcase with a half shelf of books.

They had a round rag rug as the only carpet on the floor. Clark sat on the couch looking at Mary.

"So," he said.

Mary nodded at him and sat down on the far side of the couch from the chair he sat in.

"So," he said again.

Mary kept her gaze out the window at the front lawn, the whitewashed fence with a crow grooming himself on it—provided it was a he-crow, she had no idea how to tell a she-crow from a he-crow—the highway with its row of telephone poles and long dangling line and then everything faded into the fog that had been hanging around for the last hundred weeks.

"So, Mary," he finally said. As if he had found what he had been trying to say.

She looked at him and he sat on the front of the seat. He held his hands clasped. He had parted his hair on the right side. He still wore his church tie but it had come loose while he was in the basement and he hadn't tightened it back up. She blinked.

"We should do something sometime."

"I'm not sure if Margaret would like that."

"She doesn't have to know about it," he said. "Just you and me. You like to eat out?"

"Not particularly."

"Would you like to?"

Mary looked at him. He'd unclasped his hands and now had them clutched on the caps of the chair. The lace arm protectors bunched under his grip.

She looked outside again and the crow had gone on to some other business and it was just the whitewashed fence in the front yard now.

Several nights a week Jack Ramon picked Mary up and drove her to his house. He came to the porch if Roger's car was home and Roger came out and shook his hand. "Nice to see you, Mr. Carnation," he said.

Mr. Carnation accepted the handshake and looked at Mary. He didn't say anything and she never understood the significance of the look. What did he mean by looking at her without saying anything every time she went away in Jack Ramon's car?

His two kids came to the door to see her, a two-and-a-half year old who still required diaper changing and an elaborate bedtime procedure and a five-year-old who helped watch the two-year-old during the evening. Sasha, the five-year-old, came to the door wearing a feather boa and a pink dress. "Ray," she said—Ray was the two-year-old—"wants to wear this boa. I told him feathers are for girls and daddy said wrapping things around your neck is dangerous. Isadora Duncan died that way. Her scarf was long since that was her signature look, a long flowing scarf. It wrapped around the tires of her little sports car and strangled her to death. Someone said about her death, 'Affectations can be dangerous'."

"They are, Sasha," Mary said.

Aileen called when she arrived at the house. Jack answered the phone in the whirl of his wife getting ready to go out. He handed the phone to Mary, "Mrs. Carnation is on the phone for you."

Mary for some reason wanted to correct him. She wanted to say, "Her name is—" but her mother had changed her name so many times now in her life that she wasn't sure that it mattered. Only three times. It made it sound like dozens of times when she thought about it that way. What was the use of a name if it could change?

Aileen always called to remind her about some chore she'd forgotten to do.

"I will do it tomorrow, mother."

"It needs to be done every day," she said. "That's why it's a chore."

"Yes," she said. "I understand."

Mary knew the call wasn't about that, but it was about judging where she'd been between their house and the Ramon house. That Aileen didn't do this in her own house, this checking up on her, made her angry. This playing at parenting. That is what it was. The call wasn't for her. She didn't have anything to say to her and didn't even pretend she had anything to say to her. She just called so that Mr. Ramon understood that Aileen cared about her daughter enough to check on her, to keep tabs on her.

"That your mother on the phone again?" In the kitchen Mrs. Ramon drank a hot spicy tea. The room smelled like cloves and cinnamon. Mary always wanted to drink it but it was Mrs. Ramon's special tea to soothe her voice before singing. She sang at a club several nights a week. She was always drinking the tea and reading a magazine when Mary came to the house because that was Mary's job to watch the kids while Mrs. Ramon went out and sang.

"Yes, Mrs. Ramon."

"That woman calls every time to see where you've gone. How come she don't know?"

"She does know."

"Why is she calling here, then?"

Mary had nothing to say to that. To her it seemed obvious it was a ten-minute drive from the Carnation house to the Ramon house. She called twelve minutes after she left the house. Two minutes wasn't enough time to do anything; what she didn't understand is why they didn't call in the evening. They didn't know when she left and when she would come home.

"She checks on you every minute. My child's five. I don't know where she is."

In the hallway between the kitchen and the living room there were framed photographs of singers in Seattle. There was one of Frank Sinatra even. Mary didn't know who most of them were but the presence of Sinatra made them all seem more glamorous to her than maybe they were, the black suits, the mix of black, Asian, and white faces was cosmopolitan to her. There was a record on the wall with the label on it with Edna Ramon's name printed. That was her. The record indicated to Mary some tragedy. She could have been famous but wasn't because of something unforeseen that had happened; she'd become ill or maybe it was just bad luck. She had a record and people beyond this street knew who she was even if the people on this street not only didn't know who she was but thought she was just a neighborhood Mexican woman. She wasn't even Mexican, but Puerto Rican.

As soon as she arrived and as soon as the tea had been drunk, Mrs. Ramon rushed around the house getting dressed. She had no shame in front of Mary or her husband. She ran around in her underclothes, skidding on the hardwood floors, and then put on her dress but was unable to zip it until Jack stopped in the hallway and pulled up her zipper. She should have some modesty. She was on in years and her skin had a soft, dimpled texture with odd hairs coming out of her back. She wasn't hairy, really, but she had some hair on her back and Mary took the time to look at it. The first time she'd been embarrassed but now that it was the routine, she wanted to see what a woman who wasn't her mother looked like because maybe she didn't want to look like her mother when she got old. Maybe she would look like Mrs. Ramon instead. That would be a good thing, to look like Mrs. Ramon instead of her mother.

Mrs. Ramon wore long eyelashes and red—almost black—lipstick. Her eyes were outlines and before she went she stood in front of her two children in the living room. They'd been playing around the house and they knew the rhythm of the night and so they moved to the front room and played on the floor and waited for their mother and then she stood before them and raised her arms. "How do I look?"

"You look beautiful, mother," Sasha said.

And Ray started to clap his hands. This is what he'd been doing lately. He clapped his hand and she turned around for them. Mary thought she did look very interesting in her dress. She looked ready to go onto a stage and sing. Mary would like to hear her sometime. She'd looked for her record in the house, but the only copy of the record was the one in the glass frame and even though she'd examined that she didn't see any way of getting the record out of the frame.

The Ramons climbed into their car and drove away. Mary spent the evening going through the familiar cycle, drawing, playing ball on the carpet, eating dinner, washing up after eating dinner, the chasing game where they put on one of the loud jazz records in the collection and then ran around the house, and then they lay on the floor panting. It was time to put them to bed, and she brushed their teeth. Sasha helped Ray with his teeth and then Mary inspected and then finally put them to bed. Mary felt nearly alone in the Ramon's house.

The kids went to sleep immediately. From the stories of the other babysitters at school, this made the Ramons a desirable babysitting gig.

Mary took the frame of the record down and turned

it over to see if she could remove it without breaking anything. It looked like she could. It was secured with a number of bendable tabs on the back. She bent them. One of them broke off. She cut her finger on another one. She pulled the board out and the record was stuck in a kind of cardboard sleeve. She took it out and almost dropped it. She placed it on the turntable and then played it.

It was a torch song but had a long bit that was very soft and then the chorus came very loud and Edna Ramon pulled her voice back into the back of her throat.

My man don't come home late at night.

He don't come home early in the morning

I don't know where he is. The truth?

The truth is he best stay away.

She listened to the song several times and then was afraid they'd come home. She heard them, she thought, and then hurriedly put it away and the record dropped on the side of the sofa. It didn't break. She picked it up and then it tipped down onto the hard wood floor and snapped. She picked it up and it seemed okay. But when she put it back into the frame, it wasn't okay. It was broken in two. A very fine line. She fit them together and then put the whole thing back together again and put it up against the wall.

There were keys in the door and Mr. Ramon came into the house without Mrs. Ramon.

Mary was flushed from the record.

He stopped and then went over and turned off the stereo.

"How were the kids?" he asked.

"Good," she said. "The kids are good."

He went to the bedroom to check on them. She watched him lean down to kiss them on their cheeks.

"I'll give you a ride home."

"But who'll listen out for the kids?" She didn't know where Mrs. Ramon was.

"They're sleeping," he said. "The drive there and back is twenty minutes."

She wanted to go home. So she believed him. She didn't really believe him but she didn't want to stay here any longer.

He checked on his children again. "They are dead asleep," he said.

He locked the door to the house. He opened the door for her. The car smelled like smoke. He grunted when he sat down in the seat next to her and he turned and smiled at her. "Thank you for taking care of my kids," he said.

He handed her the envelope with her money it, like he always did when he drove her home.

On the drive he said, "She wanted to be a star, you know?"

"Mrs. Ramon?"

"She is one. A star is hard to live with. For a while before the kids were born I thought she would make it. I thought that. She cut a 45 and it did well. She got a lot of work for that and for a year it looked like she actually had done it. It was just a matter of time. She sang Vegas, LA, you name it. People knew who she was."

He started the car and backed it out onto the highway and began to drive. Mary didn't know where Mrs. Ramon was; why hadn't she come back like she always had?

"That was her best year," he said. "During a year like that we both thought given a year like this the rest will be gravy."

The road turned over a deep gully and the angles of the road were sharp. He drove onto a shoulder and then slowed the car down. Only then did she realize that he was drunk. Only in his driving did she realize that, because his speech was fine. He seemed tired, that was all, but in his driving, his lack of attention to where they were on the road, he was drunk, she knew.

"But a person can't live on gravy. The year ran out and nothing ever really came of the record besides the record. The record was out there but there was no one asking about a second record. Well, people asked about the second record, but no one who would make a second record happen asked about it.

"We sent them stuff. But they weren't asking and weren't interested in what we sent."

He rolled the window down and let in the damp air from outside, the smell of rotting leaves on the shoulder, and then they passed over the bridge near her house. It smelled of the rotting salmon.

"She holds it against me and sometimes lets herself get talked into thinking it will happen again for her. She was twenty-five then. She's not past it yet, but you know every year she gets further away from that year. Something could happen, I guess. I just don't think it will happen with me. I don't think she believes that."

Mr. Ramon turned to look at Mary and he shrugged. "I had my chance."

He stopped the car and Mary quickly climbed out. "Please drive home safely, Mr. Ramon," she said.

She thought about the children and what if he didn't get back. When she got back to the house, Roger Carnation was watching from the living room.

He had a cup of coffee and one of the historical novels he always read.

"Mary?" he said.

She turned to look at him and then went up the stairs to where he wasn't allowed. She took off her clothes and put on her pajamas and brushed her teeth and then lay down in her bed and lay completely still in an approximation of sleep. She wanted to call to find out if he got home safely.

When she called in the morning, Mrs. Ramon answered the phone her voice angular and raspy in the early morning.

"Is everything all right?" Mary asked.

"Why wouldn't it be?" Mrs. Ramon said.

Martha

Clark could do it. But he might not get away with it because he was not in the family and if someone inside the family did it, if they rid them of Roger Carnation, then he would be gone. She thought about it. She didn't want it to be a long drawn out thing, his death, but she wanted it be something that happened and then he would be dead. Aileen would get the money from the insurance company. Did they have to have a body to get the insurance money? Maybe they could just take a body part—his severed head—and roll it into a field. What could they find out from a severed head? They wouldn't think that the family had killed him if they cut off his head. They would think he had enemies. A man such as Roger Carnation must have enemies who would cut off his head. Martha would cut off his head. There must be others. His enemies were his own family. He couldn't escape from his enemies. They would dig his grave with their bare hands and see him into it.

She could make Roger Carnation tremble and this trembling she at first thought when he came to her and she knew what he wanted would be a source of her power over him. She made him tremble and shake and at first she thought, well then, she had power over him because he would tremble and shake and she would make him stutter and his hands jostle like she had run a voltage through his bones. She transformed him from an old man into something else, something that needed this transformation. She knew then after that fist time—they had just moved to the house and her mother had started to go out, to complain that Roger Carnation was always at her and she didn't need to have anything coming at her at her age—her mother was just thirty-three years old, was that so old? Martha thought it was very old. Not old like old age old but old in that her mother had a right to do what she thought she needed to do. Martha didn't have a right and she thought by making this trade, by doing what Roger Carnation required, that things would work out, that she would have some control over him and this control would allow her to not do it or to do it rarely.

It did work out that way at first. He was unsure after she had taken him out and then sucked and licked and sucked until he shuddered and the bitter, salty stuff come out of him and she swallowed what this was, this stuff that should not be coming out of this man who in general played at being her father but was not her father so they weren't doing anything unredeemable before the eyes of Jesus, but they weren't doing something that couldn't be easily explained either. She had no passion in relation to Roger Carnation but rather desired to have power over him and she thought this bargain may be worth it at first, because after she did this thing, he did not touch her as Orton had touched her. He did not want to saddle up next to her. Instead he sat down on her bed and she left the room and went into the bathroom and brushed her teeth and rinsed her mouth out and gargled and put toothpaste in the water and gargled and then brushed her teeth again and then she looked at herself in the mirror and knew she wanted to cry but she could not cry because then she would not have the power over him that she had wanted. This was why she had done it. If she came out and she had tears in her eyes he may still be hungry and then he would know what he did and if he knew what he did then there would be no boundaries around what he wanted and she could deal with these boundaries.

She smiled and walked out of the bathroom and Roger Carnation fled the room. She followed him. "Where are you going, poppa?" she asked. "What's downstairs when you could be upstairs?"

"Doesn't anything bother you?" he said from the bottom of the stairs. He said this in a low, growling voice. "What you just did."

"Do you want me to never do that again?"

He didn't say anything and when he closed the door she felt she had won. She went to her room and wanted to cry but then she realized, why cry over something like that? She had taken him. She felt at that moment like she owned him.

And so it seemed. What did he really want? He wanted that fluid taken out of him. That is what he wanted. He wanted that teaspoon of fluid sucked out like puss.

For a week after this, then, Roger Carnation did not bother her. He bought her, secretly, a new dress that she didn't like and it was too small, although she could fit into it.

Her mother's mood improved as well. Her mother's mood improved, Martha thought, because he wasn't at her anymore. He didn't care about her anymore. He'd moved on to something new. Her mother was no longer then the woman of the house. She was the only woman, now. The only job with authority in the household she had given up. Her mother was a housecleaner then. Her mother was the help. Her mother was the cook. She wasn't a good cook, but good help was trouble to find these days.

Martha noticed that he wouldn't come up the stairs unless she was the only one home. He wouldn't come up the stairs, and she would go there to deprive herself of him. A week later she wore the dress he'd bought her and he took her into the trailer outside. He took her outside and she walked across the damp yard in the drizzle with him.

The lights were on in the trailer, the whirling motion lamp, and they climbed the stairs and she did what she'd done before. He seemed shocked again and simply allowed what needed to happen to happen. This time she spit him out onto the floor and then went back inside, leaving him a little limp and spent in the trailer. She didn't like the privacy of the space. She preferred the uncomfortable, stolen privacy of the living room where it had first happened. She didn't know what could happen in the trailer.

The trailer, though, became a regular fixture and for months then a regular rhythm developed. She would visit him and perform her chore and then leave him there inside the trailer and then he wanted to see her naked.

"I don't want to get naked," she said.

He started to grab her clothes and so she stepped back and out of the trailer. "I won't come into the trailer again," she said.

And that is when her power in the situation dissolved. She was surprised how quickly he moved, but he moved very quickly out of the trailer and grabbed her. "I don't want," she said.

"You will," he said.

He took her back into the trailer. She tried to scratch him and she squirmed, and he held her and she bucked her legs and then he held her down against her neck.

"You'll leave bruises on my neck," she said. "Everyone will know."

"Don't move then," he said.

She struggled and he held her down and she could feel what he was doing between her legs. He had her legs open and then she felt the cold floor on her butt as he pulled down her panties. He held her down and then she started to see white stars skip across her field of vision. The lantern turned around and around and he put something cool and damp against her legs, something that smelled odd, like engine oil, like something that shouldn't be between her legs. She tried to scream and she could hear the sound coming out of her mouth but it wasn't a sound really but the intent of a sound that was blocked by his hand on her throat and then she woke then to find him red-faced and sweating between her legs. He had taken the top of her dress and it was bunched around her stomach and he was working on her back and forth and back and forth and then he stopped and pulled himself out of her and she felt the throbbing emptiness of where he'd been. He rubbed himself. His entire hand grasped the shaft of his penis and his other hand toggled the tip of his penis and then the stuff came out: so little for so much effort. Tiny drops of it splattered on the floor in front of him and then a long, squiggly arc splattered onto her stomach. He made a grunting noise like something had happened to him. He was done.

"Get dressed," he said.

She pulled her clothes back on and went upstairs and drew her bath. It wasn't her night for a bath and Mary hammered on the door.

"Martha, it's not fair."

"I need to soak it off," she said.

"It's my turn for a bath. I'm telling mom."

"What are you going to tell her?"

Her mother came to the door and said, "It isn't your turn for a bath," she said. "Unlock the door."

She unlocked the door and there was her mother and Mary and they could see her with bruises around her neck. She could see them looking at the shape of those marks: Roger's fingers. "What is it?" she asked.

Her mother said, "Mary, let her have the bath." And they closed the door. She finished her bath and then went back to her room. Her mother knew. Did she know before? What would she do now?

She went downstairs and Roger Carnation still hadn't come into the house. Her mother didn't say anything to her. What was there to say? There were only things to do, but she didn't do anything.

"You need to wear a turtleneck for a couple of days."

"I was wearing a scarf. I was outside and I was wearing a scarf."

"I told you not to do that," she said.

"You are always looking out for me," Martha said.

"You'll get killed doing stuff like that," she said. "There was that actress who strangled herself on her scarf."

"You stopped wearing your scarf," Martha said. "And now I have to."

"What is that supposed to mean?"

"I don't know."

"You wear something over your neck, lest people get ideas."

She no longer had the illusion that she had power over him after that or even that if her mother found out there would be hell to pay. Even this she became used to. He didn't always want this, but he said he wanted to have more of a catalog of things she would be willing to do. He didn't like it when she tried to think of something new. She didn't like it when he thought of something new but she accepted that she had to learn what he wanted her to do.

When he finally tired of her, he moved on to Mary. Mary returned to bed one night. Her bathrobe was still open. She had her pajamas on and she lay down in the bed and didn't say anything and Mary new. She knew, too, that Roger had gone right for what he wanted with Mary and that there had been none of the building up.

She knew Mary knew about her. And in the darkness then that night, Mary turned to her and asked her, "Are you not doing that anymore?" she asked.

"He doesn't want it anymore."

"I'm sorry," she said.

"What are you sorry for?"

"I'm sorry that I was angry at you for letting him to do it to you."

"You were angry at me?"

"I thought you were doing it because you wanted to do it."

"I thought if I did it, I would at least know what was happening."

"Why doesn't Mom do anything?"

"For the same reason you didn't do anything. She's scared. She doesn't want to have what happened before happen again."

"But why did she marry him?"

"Because he does things for us. Because he provides a roof over our heads."

"That's like the hens thanking the farmer for giving them a place to live."

They started to laugh. "How could this happen to a family twice?"

They lay in the darkness and then Martha said it. "We can do something about it. No one will question why we did it."

"What can we do?"

"We can kill him."

"With what?"

"One of his rifles."

"Who? Are you going to shoot him?"

"Marshall."

"I'm more likely to kill someone than Marshall."

"Clark, then."

"Clark isn't going to kill anyone."

"Marshall will. Marshall hates him as much as we do."

"If we kill him," Mary said, "Mom'll just marry another man, same as, maybe even worse, than the old."

"We won't let her."

Martha asked Marshall to come out with her and Clark. They were going to go to the quarry on Highway 18 and shoot Clark's rifle and handgun. "It'll be a blast," she told him. "Pun intended." Marshall sat in the closet upstairs that he had made into his study. He'd hung a sheet over the entrance and going inside he had a light bulb he'd painted with designs turned on, and over his desk he had a bright engineering lamp. He worked on his math problems at his desk and read books while sitting on the floor and drinking coffee. He had a small radio tuned to a Brahms. He didn't like symphonic music but of all the noise he could get out of the radio this was the only one he could tune out. Mary, though, sometimes heard him listening to the top forty countdown. When she knocked he would have turned the station to the classical music station. It bothered her that she couldn't listen to the music as well with him. Sometimes she stood outside and listened to the channel and she could hear hardly audible music. She could hear Marshall's whisper chanting the words to the songs. *Don't leave your gum on the bedpost overnight.*

Mary wasn't asked to go the quarry.

Marshall of course said no. "I don't believe in firearms. If a person wants to kill someone else they should have to do it with their bare hands. Embrace the barbarism of killing others."

The three of them knew why Martha asked Marshall. She asked Marshall because he said he would kill Roger. She asked Marshall because Marshall had said he would kill him if his two sisters asked him and now she was asking him to get some practice with a handgun.

"Do I have to tell you why I'm asking you?" Martha asked. She asked him in her arch voice, the one she had lifted from their mother.

Marshall said, "I'll get my coat. There must be a better way to do this."

"It's what people do," Martha said, as if that settled that. As if, "Don't be silly." And Clark stood on the porch wearing his black slacks and a wool turtleneck sweater. Clark shook Marshall's hand when he came out of the house. "Nice that you'll come along."

Marshall nodded and sat in the backseat on his hands and looked to Martha like he was being taken off to his own execution.

Clark sped down the dusty asphalt highway. It had just rained and now the sun was out and clouds lifted up from the fields and the pavement. Water sprayed up onto the windshield and little spectrums flashed briefly in the mist zipping around the car.

"I thought about signing up," Clark said in a loud voice back to Marshall. "I thought about joining the Marines. I even went down to the recruiting station and looked into it. They said though that someone with my build would probably end up with a desk job. Just too slight. Have you thought about it?"

"I have tried not to think about it. There's no reason to join the Army. I don't want to kill anyone."

"They say killing a man is a rite of passage. You can't really be a man until you've killed someone. Woman, she gives birth to a man. Man, he takes it back. It's all very primal."

"I don't think it's as easy as that," Marshall said.

"It's easy. People try to make it more complicated than it is. That's the wonderful thing about this country. We've started to strip everything down to the basics. When you get a plate of American food, for example, you know what you've got. A cut of meat. Some vegetables. A little butter. Some potatoes. We are real. You get yourself some French food and you don't know what it is. Could be anything."

"That analogy doesn't make very much sense to me," Marshall said. "If you're saying Americans are more primitive than other people, you're not going to get any argument from me. We took a perfectly good continent with perfectly civilized people and made it a wilderness. But if you are trying to say we are *real*, that's bullshit. Realism is a European invention. Allegory is the only reality Americans understand. George Washington, Washington Irving, Hawthorne, Melville, Elvis, and Kennedy."

Clark looked into the rearview mirror to see if Marshall was making fun of him or kidding around but Marshall was looking out at the dairy fields.

Carnation

Roger Carnation started attending church in Basic Training to remind him of home although he rarely went to church when he was home. Instead, before his mother rounded up Roger's two brothers, Roger walked up to the upper pasture and waited until the car left. He drove the Ford tractor down to the house to change the oil, which he liked to do on a Sunday when he could sit on the grass and listen to the engine oil drip into the pan. The black fluid slowly filled the bucket. He punctured the silver canister with the dusty half U of the spigot and poured it back into the engine. The old oil filled the drum and sometimes on Sundays he took the drums to the dump. He poured the oil over the garbage. If he could, he set the oil on fire as he left. He didn't smoke, so he had to remember to bring a match. He threw out the match and watched the flames jump up, blue flames at first and then a thick black smoke. He drove out before the junk man at the gate saw what had happened. He came back home on Sunday having done all of that before his mother and brothers came back from Church with their white shirts, dark slacks, and thin black Sunday jackets. Roger Carnation wore his work clothes splattered in oil. His mother didn't say anything and then when they sat down at the table and said grace, Roger, with his head down, looked at the plate. He could see his shadowy head in the surface as he held his two bothers' hands and looked sideways up from his head at the steam coming up from the mashed potatoes. As soon as grace was over, before he even put the potatoes on his plate, he broke the skin on the gravy and poured it across the plate. His mother said, "You need potatoes before you take gravy." She asked, "How come you don't go to church with us anymore? You used to go." Finally she said, "Barbara asks about you every Sunday." Roger knew that Barbara and he might have been going steady if he still went to church but the whole thing with Barbara bothered him because she wore a shawl sometimes and wore her hair like her mother's—up on her head in a long bun—and even though he could imagine it coming out and then all over her shoulders he didn't like it because when he did talk to her and spent time with her she bought him a white shirt and wanted him to wear it and he couldn't wear a white shirt because it didn't stay white for very long. His wearing a shirt turned the shirt speckled. So he wore plaid shirts he could afford to throw away if the stains didn't come out. The stains were difficult to see anywhere in a plaid shirt. Besides, Roger didn't think Barbara, with her heavy waist, long forearms, and her squashed nose, was as interesting as she herself thought she was. Roger found himself at school following down the hallway behind a thin, black-haired girl who lived in Colville. Her father owned the laundry and employed

Filipinos and she wore pleated dresses and white shirts with lacy collars and no one said anything about her. No one knew her father who worked in the laundry, but he followed her. Barbara had noticed at lunch one day Roger sitting alone and watching this girl, that he was watching her and that was it, she stopped bringing him pieces of pie from home. And going to church wasn't even fun because Barbara didn't sit in the corner and talk to him after that and so he stopped going to church.

His brothers went to Eastern Washington University to study agriculture and Roger had every plan to go but as soon as he graduated he was drafted into the Navy.

That dusty weekend after the paper arrived in the mailbox, after school let out, after the Fourth of July parade, when the parade ground still had hay on it, Roger walked into town and past the laundry. The front windows had boards across them. It was the shadowy side of the street and the other side was in the sun and an old man sat on bench with his face in the sun and his hat on his lap. The man had his face up and his eyes closed. Down a little farther the barbershop had a few people in it, and there were a few cars in the parking spots but otherwise the street was empty except for the warm dry wind that smelled like dry grass and dust. Visible on the next block he saw the clock in front of the jeweler's; it was a giant city style clock like a lamppost. 10:35. He walked into the laundry and the girl was sitting on a chair reading a schoolbook. The book was thick with thin, glossy pages and a binding covered with a brown paper bag. She looked at him and he smiled at her. "Do you have the time?"

She got up. She set the book on the counter and lifted the swinging counter to step through. She smiled again at him, exposing pretty straight teeth except for her front teeth which overlapped slightly. She had thin legs and bulgy knees like paper stuffed into socks. Her skin was brown and had a light fur. She wore her same clothes. She walked out into the middle of the sidewalk and squinted at the Main Street clock in front of the jewelry store. She took out a pair of glasses that had been in her front dress pocket, visible on the arch of her hip. She took them out, uncrossed the legs and tucked the legs behind her ears. "10:37" She turned back and went into the store and smiled at him.

"What's your name?"

"Roger Carnation."

"You just graduated."

"I did."

She nodded her head and then took off her glasses and tucked them back into the tight pocket on her hip. She and Roger stared at the ad for Martinizing. Billboards covered the front of the counter and were taped to the inside windows. "Do you need something Martinized?"

Having her in front of him then, directly, he could see she was older than he had imagined. She had a rim of thick blackish hair over her upper lip, not a mustache, but the kind of growth old maids get. She studied him, he could see, with a sort of quick roving look. Her pupils jiggled as she took him in.

"I've been drafted," he said as a way of explaining. He knew he should tell Barbara but she would want to do something about it, formalize their relationship in some way, take a ring or get engaged or even if they had enough time go somewhere like Spokane without anyone knowing they'd gone and he didn't want to do that.

"Oh?"

"Into the Navy."

"That should be safer," she said.

"Safer?"

"Than the Army. My brother is in the Army. He says it

is very dangerous."

"You have a brother?"

"He's in Africa." She fiddled with the stem of her glasses in her pocket, adjusting them on her hip. "It sounds more exotic than it is. Sounds like a Tarzan movie or something. But really it's just desert. He says it's like Arizona."

"Arizona sounds good to me."

"It isn't," she said. She looked around the shop and then smiled at Roger Carnation. "Well, if you don't need any dry cleaning, I need to get back to work or my dad will kill me if he sees I'm talking to strange men who've wandered off the street. He won't allow me to go on the other side of the counter."

She ducked back under the counter. "Are you sure you don't need anything?"

"No," he said.

"Here," she said. "Do you like green, orange, or yellow?"

"What?"

"Lollipops?"

She offered him a box with packets of cellophane-wrapped candy, each one a pellet of translucent candy with a curved waxy stem like a loop. They looked to Roger like baby bickies.

"What flavor are they?"

"Green is green. I think it's supposed to be apple but it just tastes like it tastes. Yellow is supposed to be lemon. And orange is supposed to be orange."

"Green."

He went to church to remind him of home and he liked the Navy churches because they didn't seem like real churches, just the idea of a church, a box with a steeple and bell and white cross. The chaplains preached to a generic god using a generic bible and Roger went to the church in basic training on Sundays to sit still while the other swabbies cleaned the barracks. He trained in San Diego and then left for a submarine. He kept going to churches when he got out because he liked them and he liked having something to do on Sundays and churches always had lots of young girls.

Roger served in the Navy until Korea in 1953 when he went to France where his lack of imagination—to him imagination was pretension—and his ideals, got in the way of him having a good time. In France Roger wanted to escape his provincialism and become somebody. All of the Americans he met in France had artistic aspirations and he didn't. They all wanted to paint or write and in some cases they actually did these things. He didn't fit in. He preferred drinking in the bars and riding his bicycle and finding prostitutes. So he returned to the US after a year of France. He spoke French with an odd, garbled accent. He returned and went to the University of Washington and served in the Navy Reserve and finally graduated and found a job with the Naval Base in 1958. He wore a suit and slacks and a hat to work. And that particular day he was looking forward to the homecoming football game even though he didn't go to the high school and didn't play the game in high school, in the Navy, the Army and Navy game became something of a fixture for him, something he marked the years with, a time when he watched the game and the struggle of the players. MacArthur took great interest in the game, it was known. He thought about the game during the day of the game.

He drove, then, a Pontiac with white leather seats that'd yellowed in the Eastern Washington sun and then turned green in the damp outside the rooming house where he lived in Skyway. He walked to work in the morning and then passed the car on the way back home. He drove the car to his parents' farm in Eastern Washington when he took long weekends, which he took every so often. Most of the time he worked and then came home and read Westerns. He went to church and then they asked him to go to the picnic at Flaming Geyser State Park and he went.

He followed the girl who was flirting with the pastor. He followed her past the heavy picnic tables full of watermelon and fried chicken. He followed her. She was looking at him. "How do you do?"

"Who are you here with?"

"I am here with Charles. You know him?"

"Is he as old as you? Because if he is I'm sure I don't know. I'm sure about that."

"I don't know," she said. "Excuse me.

She led him across the lawn. Families sat on blankets. The men in blue jeans with the cuffs rolled up playing horseshoes.

The girl wore a yellow dress and a yellow scarf around her head. The dark strands of hair, black and curly at the base of her neck grew longer on the top of her head and turned faint and blond at the long arc where they turned under the scarf and had yellowed in the sun. She had thick, crisp crow's eyes. Her lips had shriveled a little but were red. She sucked on her lips as she talked, leaving a shimmering, wet sheen on them and then she laughed. Her shoulders had the width of a boy's shoulders. He could see the flexing bones of her shoulder blades under the smooth, brown skin dotted with darker brown moles. Roger didn't know Martha at that second. He didn't know who the girl was. He really only saw her as a movement. She was a fluttering walk without her shoes. Her blue saltwater sandals swung in one hand and her other hand reaching out to touch the man she talked to on the shoulder. She stood in a crowd of boys from the church, the sons of the older men who worked in the lumberyard on Lake Washington, or for the county dump in Maple Valley, workmen, and turned around with her sandals. They wore blue jeans and loose Hawaiian shirts with white T-shirts on underneath. They wore battered old work boots and shoes. The man she talked to said something and jumped back. He jumped back, shuffling his brown shoes in the straw grass kicking up dust clouds and chaff. He said to the girl, "We've already all gone out with you, Martha. What else is there?"

The dust he kicked up clouded around her, coating her legs with a film of grass particles and dirt. You're getting dust on me, she said. The other boys laughed and they all started doing a shuffling dance kicking up a large cloud.

She laughed a hoarse, hard laugh and began to walk away. She took a step toward the boys and coughed. Roger couldn't see her for a second in the haze of dust and dirt.

One of the boy's father's said, "Hey men, cut that out. There are people around."

Martha walked out of the cloud covered in the dust. The boys had started to walk away toward where the clouds of cooking met, greasy fumes and the odor of beer on ice. She took a step toward them and then looked back and saw Roger standing and watching her. He held up his beer. She brushed her hair and then walked away, she walked through the park and when she was halfway across the field Roger started walking after her. He kept a long way back and drank his beer. He crushed the can in his hand, a sudden contortion of his hand, and tossed the can across the dusty pasture. She passed under the dappled shadows toward the Flaming Geyser. He could see her yellow dress and then she was up the trail. He followed her. The geyser came out of a block of cement with a pipe and was natural gas and had always been burning here in the forest near the river although the plaque explained it had also been put out by the Flood of 1949. He didn't see Martha there and then he walked up the trail. It smelled like damp earth under the cool trees. He could see up through the canopy, the branches of maple trees, the hanging boughs of the fir trees. Not much up that way. He saw a fresh slide in the mud, a skid, and went down the trail. Stinging needles grew on the bank. The green plants had a thick, tar odor on the bank of the river. The river then flowed past him, a thick, brown and green color against the shadowy bank. The yellow dress hung from a snag on the side of the river.

He stood on the bank. He saw her sandals. He looked out into the riling water of the Green River, heavy rolling water with whirlpools and couldn't believe that anyone would swim in this wild water and then he saw her swimming out beyond the thick side of the river, toward the quickly roiling part of the river next to the other bank, where the river ran over large river stones. She stood in the sun and ducked down when she saw him looking at her.

He stood on the side of the bank knowing she could see him and then he walked into the forest and hid. He crouched and waited. The spot he sat on was packed and washed by the river and then the needles grew up. Old alder leaves, curled orange ovals and maple leaves, five lobes rotted away to just the web flap of the leaf lay on the mottled mud. The mud itself had a bubbled pattern and was black with tiny round holes. A black beetle with a shell like a blue almond walked between the stalks of the stinging needles. The girl worked her way upstream, her arms raised above the river, curved over her armpits and her hands brushed the rushing green surface of the river. The water crested at the skin under her armpits. She was in the sun and then she dove out into the river and executed several sloppy overhand strokes into the deep part of the river and when she was on the other side of the river she brushed herself up onto the bank and then climbed out of the river. He could see the waxy, submerged color of her body under water. She still had her underwear on, her bra and panties but the wet fabric clung to her pubic hair, a dark mass of curled hair on the draining water. She stood with her feet naked on the muddy bank and dried off with her towel and then looked around, slowly, and then slipped her panties off and he saw the flash of her pubic hair. He became really excited then. He rubbed his dick and grabbed it through his pants and he could apply pressure with the ball of his thumb to the tip over and over again. Her pubic hair seemed much sparser seen directly and he thought how much more he liked it under her damp underwear. She wrapped the towel around herself, giving him only a brief moment of looking at her. She wrung her underwear and bra, squeezing the water out, twisting and squeezing, and then she put them back on and snapped her yellow dress clean over the river. The dress, still dry and dusty from the field, cast out long fragments of grass and she slipped this on over her, dressed. Roger Carnation felt a heavy thick sensation roll from inside of himself and he felt a dampness and then the electrical shock dropped into his pelvis. She slipped her sandals on and then stripped her towel from under her dress. She tied up her dress and then walked back up the path. He waited down there in the bushes for a long time not wanting her to come back and then discover him there on the bank, and then he stood up and adjusted his underwear and walked back up the trail and then down past the Flaming Geyser and out into the sunlight. It seemed much later. The shadows lay longer. The sun was brighter and glittered just at the lip of the hill.

Roger looked for the girl in the yellow dress. He didn't know what he'd do. When he walked back to the shelter where the older men of the church grilled the meat he grabbed a beer and drank it. One of the boys who'd cast dirt on the girl was there and he wanted to ask the guy who that girl was and then he decided not to and then one of the men asked him if he'd like to meet Aileen Orton.

"Friend of yours?" Roger asked.

"She's a woman I know. You might like to meet her."

"Okay. Sounds good to me."

He introduced him to a woman sitting at a picnic table drinking a cup of coffee from a paper cup. She wore a turquoise dress, white canvas-soled shoes, and a pair of men's glasses. She stood up, brushed her skirt behind her, and offered her hand to Roger Carnation. He took her hand. "Aileen Orton," she said. Her arms jiggled a little where they disappeared into her loose dress. He could see her bra against her pale skin.

"How do you do?" He said and they talked about the area, about the spread of the tract homes in the Green River Valley, lamenting the loss of farmland. "I can't say I'm too nostalgic about it, though. I grew up on a farm, yeah?"

"I did as well. I wouldn't go back to a farm if my life depended on it. I work in an insurance office."

"I work in an office, too. I'm an engineer at Bangor, the submarine base."

"You are all engineers. You skinny guys who wear ties on Sunday. What is that, an engineer, anyway. You don't drive trains."

"We draw schematics. We design things right out of our heads. We're inventors."

"What did you invent?"

"I invented the Carnation Retro-stress Screw Assembly."

"I bet you did," she said. "I bet you did."

He stopped behind her in the middle of the dusty field and looked at her and then smiled seeing, as his father used to say, that she was beating the tar out of him. And then he leaned forward and brushed her face with the tips of his fingers. She flinched.

"You're a pretty girl."

"I'm no girl, Mr. Carnation."

"Mr. Carnation—" he was about to say call me Roger and then decided he liked to be called Mr. Carnation.

She smiled and then he followed her. She said. "I was married, you know."

"A woman your age already widowed?"

"Divorced."

He looked back at his congregation, playing horseshoes and thought about going back and just letting this woman go back to where she came from and then he saw the girl in the yellow dress sitting next to a girl wearing blue jeans cut to the calves. The girl stood up and said something to Aileen.

Roger Carnation hurried up and introduced himself to her offered hand. Her hair was still a little damp. But her dress looked even cleaner. She didn't have her shoes on.

"Martha, this is Mr. Carnation."

"How do you do?"

"You're a pretty young girl."

"I'm older than that," she said. "I'm a woman."

"I'm sure you are," he said.

"Mary, this is Mr. Carnation."

"How do you do?"

He looked at Mary. She was prettier than Martha, he decided, but both girls on looking at them were handsome women, strong jaws and round faces, heavy, thick noses. But Martha had plucked her eyebrows and wore a little makeup, not much, and Martha had a way of standing, sort of floating toward Roger Carnation while Mary took a measured step back and stared at Roger Carnation right in the eye. Martha didn't even look at his face, but kept one ear pointed at him. He talked directly into her ear. The hair around the ear, bleached and curled. Mary, on the other hand, wore her hair short and it already had gray hair in it and made her look at first glance much older even than her mother. She had on denim slacks and wore a T-shirt with a wide U over her chest, and a plaid, short sleeve shirt.

"Where's Marshall?" Aileen asked.

"He went for a hike," Mary said.

"I have a son, Marshall. You'll like him. Most men like Marshall. He's a bright boy."

"He's smart," Martha said.

Roger Carnation sat down and talked to Aileen but he watched as Mary and Martha played and he thought well, a divorced woman and two daughters, three for the price of one. At first it was a sort of half thought coming into his head, like my she really wasn't so pretty up close, Martha, and he had seen her submerged in the water and now he had her up close and he thought, well then, he really liked what he saw of her anyway. She had thin wrists and skinny arms tanned in the sun and she stopped occasionally to brush her hair out of her face. Mary, even prettier, had a sort of nervous, harsh movement to her arms and legs. She stood playing with Martha on both feet and then leaned in to grab the ball with her entire body rather than just plucking the ball out of the air like Martha.

"It was a pleasure to meet you, Aileen," Roger said. "Would it be all right if I called you later this week and maybe we could have dinner?"

"Mr. Carnation, that would be wonderful."

He took her to dinner and rather than being an awkward dinner, Aileen fell right into talking. Perhaps he was really deeply attracted to her because he could get his hands on the two daughters who were at that time thirteen years old and fourteen years old and he sat there drinking a bottle of soda and laughing with her and he kept his eye on Martha and then he began to take Aileen out for dinner. They went to the Rose Gardens and the Botanical Gardens; he had a passion for the Rose Gardens. She liked walking slowly with them through the place while he held his booklet from the Washington State Horticulture Society and looked at the roses, reaching out and pulling a petal from a rose. They drove to the Skagit valley to look at tulips, this was the following spring after a winter of dating and there in a field of tulips he asked her to marry him.

The Hole in the Forest

Marshall

As Marshall bikes up the hill toward the house, he can see the light on upstairs. The light fades as the damp fog settles on the fields. At dusk sometimes the air made the ground cool. A wind works the tops of the trees. Marshall wonders where the wind stops? He pedals into the stand of trees where the house sits. The sharp edge of pinecone silhouettes on a waving pine bough blocks the house window for an instant. Marshall rolls into the depression before the house. The bike rattles down the slope. His hair stands. The air is cold. The creek smells of algae in the duck pond where the ducks no longer live. Instead, there are Canadian geese on the shore in the spring and fall and now they are gone. They are loud when they are there. But right now there is nothing except the wind in the trees. Marshall kicks the pedal with a metallic cling. He stands on the pedal and the bike shoots across the bridge. Roger Carnation and he spent last summer rebuilding the other side. Marshall wants to catch air on the other side.

The gully holds sword ferns and Devil's Club and always smells of cedar needles and clay. White and silver moths flutter in the shadows of the gully.

That summer they worked the bridge over the gully Marshall discovered he could have liked Roger Carnation. It was possible that if he hadn't already been his stepfather and if the things that had already been going on hadn't been going on and his mother had taken more care in introducing him into their lives, then maybe he might have been acceptable as a stepfather. But, by that summer it was too late. As soon as Roger pulled into the driveway home from work, Marshall brought him the shovels and cold coffee in a heavy glass jar and they walked down the road to the stand of fir trees below the house and worked on the bridge. They lifted the old timber and built a plywood frame to pour cement. Roger didn't speak while he worked, but began slowly and then began to get his back into it. Working alongside him, Marshall liked the slow, steady movement of the shovel and the pickaxe. They rarely talked about what they needed to do. They spent the time from the moment Roger arrived from work laboring until dusk and they couldn't see anymore. At first, it was just a couple of hours. A few weeks into June it was until late, four or five hours, and when the white moths fluttered out and they couldn't see, Roger joked about getting the car and working under the headlights like a couple of hoodlums burying a body. And then they went inside and Marshall was too tired to even eat dinner but washed off and climbed into bed. The sheets felt soft, and he ran his feet back and forth back and forth until they began to feel warm and smooth. He held onto that moment of complete tiredness in a solid, clean bed looking out into the faint blueness of the dusky summer sky. The room still held the last of the summer day heat that smelled like matchsticks. When they finished the bridge, Marshall had an odd feeling of having done something permanent. He had built the bridge, the connection of the house to the highway.

As he rides over the bridge, down from the edge of the creek valley, he pedals so fast the bike spins over the macadam they set on the bridge surface and rolls smooth with a thick roller. The bike whizzes over the surface back into the potholes and rocks of the dirt road and then Marshall loses his stomach. The bike jumps over the lip of the creek gully and rolls down the driveway through the mown grass field where Roger keeps saying they need to keep a milk cow.

The lights are on, which can only mean his sisters are upstairs and they only go upstairs this time of day when Roger drinks until drunk. He promised Aileen he wouldn't drink until drunk in the presence of her children and for him to drink until drunk only means that she is gone.

Marshall throws himself off his bike, grabs the trombone case. He keeps the bike rolling, and he lets the weight of the case carry him onto the lawn. He shifts under the weight, settling the case on the porch. The porch shudders. His bike rolls across the lawn in front of the house to the shed. He has been working on the maneuver since last school year started.

He leaves the trombone on the porch and glances in the dark windows and can't see Roger. Maybe Roger is in the camper? Marshall opens the shed door. Inside smells like mouse droppings, engine oil, the lining of the old car seats Roger hung from the rafters. Sparrows have pulled the seat contents out in the stringy-white stalactites of fluff.

Roger stands on the porch without shoes or socks on. His feet look bright red. He holds the trombone case and snaps the latch.

"You shook the house. Don't knock it off the foundation playing around like that."

"It just sits on a foundation, then?" Marshall asks.

Roger glances up from the case. "Are you talking back to me, son?"

"I'm talking," Marshall says. "I don't know in what direction, backwards or forwards."

"You shouldn't talk back to your superiors. That's a lesson they still teach. I know they teach that." Roger finds the lock clip and snaps the case open. He lifts out the trombone. He runs his hand over the plush felt liner. He finds the latch for the mouthpiece. He takes out the mouthpiece. Marshall stands on the damp grass. It is his job. In the fall, he stops as soon as it starts to get damp. The grass still grew, and now the blades of grass are as thick and heavy as spaghetti noodles and soak the cuffs of his jeans. Martha stands at the upstairs window. She's been standing there for a moment. He saw her before, he remembers. She stood in her long dark dress. The yellow room light behind her attracts glittering moths from the forest, mosquitoes, and jack o' spanners. She makes some kind of gesture to him. He can just see her elbow working behind the shadow. Her arms are dark in the shadows. Marshall doesn't spend time looking at her. He knows not to make as if he sees her. He half wants Roger to try to play the trombone because he's never played it before, and then he would fail to play it and see that he knows that for Marshall to play at least requires some kind of skill.

Roger holds the mouthpiece. He finds the tube to insert. He inserts it into the horn.

"Roger, I don't think that is a good idea."

"Show me how to play this thing," Rogers says.

Marshall climbs onto the porch. The porch is exposed in the weather. Even though Roger painted it four—or now five summers ago—The paint now scatters flecks on the porch and crunches under Marshall's feet. The boards have shrunk and silvered. Every now and then, Roger goes out with a hammer to pound the nails back into the wood. The edge of the metal hammer leaves rings of broken wood grain in the boards. Marshall's stepfather smells of beer and table pepper. Marshall keeps an arm's length from the old man. He wants to be able to jump before Roger lunges at him. He opens the screen door. No one has started a fire. The house has the cold smell it possesses when it has been closed all day; there is no one to keep it home-like. No one has cooked anything, nor has the lit fire driven the musty outdoors smell out. The living room smells like the shed: mold spores, leaves, and mud. Roger manages to get a solid blast from the horn. The note comes out as a thick bass honk. And then Roger begins to make the noise over and over. A row of bottles sits in a neat row on the lamp table beside the reading chair. The bottles glow warmly under the lamplight, but the room without the fire going is cold. The daily paper lies neatly folded, unread, on a hassock. Normally, his sisters sit at the kitchen table. His mother makes some kind of household noise somewhere in the house. There is a sound from a different room, the sewing machine, the clank of the clothes machine crank, or if Mother has everything done, she sits under the open window reading by the last of the daylight. She doesn't like to turn on the lights. She says she doesn't like to turn the light on because she grew up in a home without electricity, just kerosene; she doesn't like bulb light. When Marshall turns the bulbs on, Mother follows him around the house and turns them off. Not right behind him. He never actually caught her turning the lights off, but if he left a room and came back, the light would be off unless she was asleep. She never left the house, tonight being the exception. It is a big deal, he realizes, and not something he ever really thought about before, her turning the lights off like that. It is her room, he figured, because she is in it. If the daylight fades, they would move closer and closer to the windows until finally she closed her book and stared into the bluish dusk. His mother knit by touch in the dark room and when finally, only after darkness sealed itself, would she say, wonderingly, "Marshall dear, can you turn on a light?" He doesn't even think she realizes she is like this. The bulbs being on in the house feel to him odd, oppressive, unsafe.

Roger stomps and marches up and down the porch, pounding out the single note he has found. Black. Stomp. Blah. Stomp.

Marshall opens the icebox and sees the crisper drawer full of black beer bottles still coated with the dust from the shed. He takes out the hot dogs and sets them on the counter. The hot dogs leak a yellowish fluid into the bottom of the package, and it sloshes on the counter. He takes the copper-bottom pot hanging from the stove and fills it with tap water. At the old house, they had to pump the water right from the ground into the sink. Marshall likes that a little more because then he knows where the water is coming from. Water from a tap came from anywhere. Well, he knows where it came from actually. But it *can* come from anywhere. This water came from the Cedar River Watershed where he'd gone fishing with Roger.

They went toward the end of the summer to go fishing in the overflow reservoir, Rattlesnake Lake. The stumps of virgin growth filled the lake bed of Rattlesnake Lake. Near the shore the silver wood came up out of the lake bottom. At first the roots were just shadows below them and then the closer to shore they got, they could see waves breaking around the wood and then they were like little islands. The mud flats exposed in the low water were studded with hundreds of stumps. Roger said trout like to hide under the stumps, that is what makes the lake such a great place to fish. He had rented a metal motorboat, but they spent most of the day drifting with the wind and casting into the clear water. "The motor scares the fish," Roger said. "Don't speak louder than a whisper." Marshall liked being out in the middle of the lake because he could see the submerged stumps through the clear water. It was clear enough to see, but cast a deep green tint under them. And then above them the sky was clear except for a few faint clouds way up above Rattlesnake Ridge. A warm wind came up the valley and the thick, frothy waves splashed into the side of the boat. A logging rail ran along one edge of the lake and at one point a train sped along, its steel wheels screeching on rusted steel rails. Roger stood up and started yelling at the train, "People are trying to fish here!"

At dusk, Marshall's skin started to hurt from being out in the wind and sun all day. It felt as if someone had run sandpaper over his face. Tiny flies moved out with the shadow of Rattlesnake Ridge. In the black water of the mountain shadow rings of jumping fish spread over the still lake. The rest of the lake still sat in the last of the sunlight and was choppy with the wind, but in the wind, shadow and the darkness of Rattlesnake Ridge the fish fed. Roger and Marshall started to catch fish. When Marshall pulled in the first fish, Roger said, "You've got a log there. That's no fish."

And then it jumped out of the water about ten yards from the boat.

"It'll take your line to the bottom and wrap it around

a stump," Roger said. "That's why they like this lake."

Marshall pulled the fish in, and Roger grabbed it and it slipped out of his hand and slithered across the hull of the metal boat. Finally, Roger held the fish and showed its blank fisheyes, like two ball bearings, to Marshall. The gills of the trout flared open exposing their inner fish workings and then closed. The fish contorted its spine one way and then the other. "He's a wiggly one," Roger said and then he whacked the fish against the side of the boat hard enough that one of the eyes flew off the head. "One down, five to go," he said.

"If we can go now you can have my fish," Marshall said.

"He's your kill," Roger said.

They fished there in the falling darkness under Rattle snake Ridge for another hour until Roger caught three more fish. And then he said, "We should go in before you build up a good sized complaint for your mommy," he said.

Steam fills the kitchen. The air becomes hot at the stove. Away from the heat, steam turns into drips of water and trickles down the wall. Steam comes out of the pot in surging bubbles, splattering boiling water on the enamel stove. Each splatter evaporates and leaves tiny rings of orange grease.

Marshall spears the hot dogs with a fork. The edge of his finger grazes the boiling water. He brushes off the heat. He puts the oily orange cylinders on a plate and taps out a smear of ketchup. Roger stomps into the house blurting honks from the trombone. *Black stomp plat.* Roger drops it with a jangle by the door. He comes to the kitchen without really looking at Marshall, and takes another beer out of the fridge. He stops and stands just over Marshall, looking down into Marshall's scalp.

"What's that you got there?"

"Hot dogs."

"That's carnival food, son. That'll give you cancer, hemorrhoids and shit knows what else. Shit. We've got real food in the freezer. Venison. Trout. Liver."

"I just want to eat my dinner and do my homework."

"Eating like that no wonder you have, spell that, S-H-I-T, grades."

Marshall takes his plate and heads for the stairs.

"Where are you going in such a hurry?"

"Leave me alone," Marshall says.

Marshall hurries up the stairs. At the top of the stairs, Martha stands holding the rifle. She looks very natural in front of the closet with the rifle at her side. She might've been standing there the entire time he was downstairs. He realizes the gesture she's been making is a sawing motion over her throat, like they might make playing cannibals. Roger is going to get his throat slashed.

"What are you doing with that?"

"If he comes up the stairs, I'm going to put a bullet straight through his chest. But now that you are home, I don't have to let it happen quickly. He's going to suffer. We're going to make him pay."

"Today?" Monday night is not a big night for crime. Not compared to Friday or Saturday when the rules of employment or school do not impose themselves at eight the following morning. People go wild on Friday or Saturday. Marshall figures that not many people died on a Monday night, and probably less died on Tuesday. If Martha has her way, they wouldn't actually do the final honors until it is Tuesday anyway. They have discussed this in the abstract. They have discussed it in concrete details. Martha once made diagrams.

Marshall sits down at his desk with his hot dogs. He feels then a temporary safety sitting at the top of the stairs. It feels warmer upstairs. The last of the warm air in the house is still up there.

"Hi, Marshall. Honey!" Roger yells up the stairs in falsetto and with their mother's intonation. "You left your trombone by the front door."

"I'll pick it up later." He doesn't want to go down through the imaginary divide of the stairs into the bright, old living room smelling of Roger's hoppy and peppery reek.

"It's going out in the yard then," Roger says.

"I'll pick it up in a minute."

"I warned you!" Marshall can hear the front door open. He rushes down the stairs. Roger has the trombone and throws it out the open door. The trombone sails down the stairs. The rim of the horn knocks the banister and the trombone flips up, and drops into the daffodil bed with a sharp clang. Marshall rushes down the steps, and Roger closes and locks the door behind him. Marshall looks up to Martha's room. She sits on her desk looking down at him.

"That is not very smart of him," she says.

A steady splattering rain comes down to soak Marshall. He finds the trombone. In the bottom tubing there is a new dent. Martha puts her pointer finger to her head, and pulls the trigger.

Marshall feels a sickness in the stomach just as he does before the first day of school. He knows his new clothes are ironed and ready to put on in the morning. His lunchbox still smells fresh and there is nothing he can do to get out of it now except go to sleep and wake up in the morning and go through with it because then the only way is to go through it. He walks around the back of the house. By the time he goes back there, his socks are soaked. The soles of his shoes squirt water out of his ankles. The back door is locked.

He sets the trombone down on its bell. He climbs onto

the deck banister and lifts himself by the gutter onto the roof. It starts to peel away with a screech. And then he is on the mossy tiles of the roof. Martha reaches out, and she pulls him into her window.

They can hear Roger Carnation downstairs. "Don't you come into the house that way. You can't come into the house without my permission. You are barred from this house! And get outside, or I'll come up there."

At the base of the stairs, Roger paces back and forth. At first, they don't think he will come up the stairs. Aileen told him he must stay downstairs. He wasn't to go upstairs anymore. She told him after she found one of his socks in Martha's room. It was one of his special dress socks, silk, with a red band. Aileen had given it to him for Christmas the first Christmas in the house. She'd been looking for the match. She finally found it, balled up and stiff under Martha's bed.

Aileen showed the sock to Martha.

"What possible use do I have with his sock?" she asked.

Martha laughed a not nice laugh until Aileen took the sock back. She set it on his chair. He did nothing. She set the sock on his lap. "Don't go upstairs," she said.

Upstairs they listened to the exchange. There was no sound from Roger. They knew then that Aileen knew. They knew she knew, but she said nothing about the entire subject; even any innuendo of her knowledge was completely off limits. They couldn't tell whether she even knew. They thought she faithfully ignored what was happening in her house. The sock was undeniable evidence, she knew. "When Mom found the sock," Mary said, "she should have stopped it." Marshall thought they all think the same thing. "She shouldn't just throw the sock at him."

Mary of course knew about the sock under Martha's bed. She says, "He won't come up because of the sock."

Martha makes a face.

"Don't say it," Mary says.

"You already know," Martha says.

"I don't need to hear it."

"He wipes his cock with it," Martha says even though they don't want to hear it. Mary looks at her and then leans into Martha. She starts to laugh and then Marshall, too, starts to laugh. At least it will soon be over.

Mary coughs. "You said..."

"I know, I said—"

"—cock."

"I did."

They start to howl with laughter.

Roger stands at the base of the stairs, and yells up to them. "Stop laughing!"

And it is this close, right then, to everything coming out in the open. All of that laughing nearly makes everything come out right then. Roger comes up the stairs. They hear the boards creak and settle.

"What are we going to do? He's coming up the stairs."

Martha leans down and picks up the rifle. "He'll get it," she whispers.

She gives the rifle to Marshall. The rifle is lighter than it seems, as if it should be heavier with its thick shining stock and oiled barrel.

"What am I supposed to do with this?"

"You know," Martha says.

The three of them are in Martha's room. The rain has stopped outside. Everything is still dripping. Water rolls off the eaves of the house. The gutters are full of cedar needles that soak up the water. A bed of moss in a thick carpet under the eaves is now soaked with water and releases the water slowly. The inside light, though, has become brighter. They can hardly see outside into the dark. Her bed is made. She has her shoes lined up under her bed. Patent leather oxfords, polished high heels, shoes Clark has given her. She's worn them once.

Marshall takes the rifle. "Are there bullets?"

"Oh, I almost forgot," Martha says. "Leave it to the last minute to ask questions like that." Marshall has Christmas morning giddiness. Nothing can go wrong because this is what life is for Christmas morning and killing stepfathers. Martha leans over and opens her pencil box and takes out a handful of bullets. "Are these the right size?" One drops on the linoleum floor and rolls across, and Mary grabs it. Marshall slips the bullet into the rifle and loads it and then he fills the magazine making a very loud metallic click with each bullet. "I think so," he says.

"I can hear you cretins," Rogers says then.

But he doesn't stick his head up.

"Martha, you come downstairs to have a beer with me, and I won't break Marshall's neck."

His voice is very loud. He is right there on the stairs.

"Fuck you," Martha says.

Mary looks sick. She looks as unhappy as Martha is happy to see Marshall holding the rifle.

"Don't you use that kind of language with me. Your mother would agree with that." He lifts himself up into the hallway between the two bedrooms. The light shines on him but he is just a silhouette. Marshall sees the corner of his cardboard toy box full of the toys he hadn't played with from before they moved into the house. He sees the crumples on his bed where Martha probably sits on his bed. She wasn't supposed to do that. Roger faces the brick chimney next to the staircase. Marshall holds the smooth wooden stock. He has the butt planted against his shoulder. He holds it the way Roger has shown him. He has his finger on the trigger. The rifle jingles just a little before he knows the stock will pound his shoulder.

Roger turns and sees that he is a sitting duck for his rifle.

"What in the hell do you think you are doing?"

"I'm going to kill you," Marshall says. When he says this he thinks it is the phrase Martha has worked out. He thinks as he says it, this is the part where I say *I'm going to kill you.*

"You can't do it." A line, Marshall thinks, right out of the movies.

Roger starts to move towards the three of them. Marshall thinks they have all seen this movie together probably.

"Marshall?" Martha says. Marshall is thinking about all of them sitting in a movie theater. Marshall spent more time looking straight up at the water stains on the ceiling of the Roxy Theater and the pillars of cigarette smoke in the light than he did watching the movie. He enjoys not watching corny old movies. "I don't know if I can do it." That's how it went in the movies and then they wrestle for the gun.

Roger brushes against the wall. Martha says something. "Shoot!" Marshall turns the tip of the rifle at Roger's leg and clicks the trigger. He hears the pin strike the head of the bullet. The force drives into his arm and his body. Smoke and the odor of cordite, crushed stone, fill the narrow space. A bright burst lights the cracks in the chimney. Roger starts to yell. Marshall flips the lever to pull another bullet into the chamber. The clack of the rifle sounds faint and tinny after the explosion.

It sounds like distant engine noises while underwater. Rogers yells. He stands against the brick chimney, howling. He doesn't have any fabric on his shoulder. His arm hangs backward. Marshall has missed his leg and hit his arm instead. Roger moves. He leans against the brick and falls. He stumbles down the stairs.

"Get him!" Martha yells.

Marshall hands the rifle to her. She holds it down at her side like an umbrella and jumps down the stairs. He watches her trundle down the stairs after Roger.

"Is he dead?" Mary asks. She has her eyes closed still.

They move down the stairs and there is another shot. "He might be dead, now," Mary says.

They find them on the front lawn. Roger is headed to the shed where he keeps his other rifles. Martha fires again. Roger stops now, out in the middle of the thick grass between the house and the shed with the antlers over the door.

Martha stands with her legs apart. She cradles the rifle in her arms.

Roger turns around to look at them.

"Marshall, call the police. Your sister has gone insane."

"Should I call someone?" Marshall asks.

"There's no need to call," Mary says. "We are in trouble if we do. He'll get away with what he's done."

"It is an accident," Marshall says.

"I'm going to kill him," Martha says. "It's either going to be here, or it is going to be where we planned."

"You can't kill me," Roger says.

"You are already dead," Martha says. "It's just a matter of your breathing and your heart beating which we will stop.

"They are going to kill you if I don't," Marshall says.

"Do you have everything?" Martha asks.

"I'll go get it," Mary says.

Roger is suddenly changed. He looks at the ground and looks pathetic standing on the wet grass with a shoulder blown away and blood running down the side of his body, and his hand twisted back away from his torso. "Just take me to the hospital. I can tell them it was an accident. No one has to get in trouble."

"Listen to him now," Martha says. "'Trouble', he says. As if we care about getting in trouble now."

"This pretty much evens us out, doesn't it?" he asks.

"It doesn't even begin to even things out," Martha says. "I should stick this rifle up your ass and then fire it."

Roger just looks at them. He turns. He starts to run towards the shed.

Martha runs after him, and then trips him. He falls on his arm, a rolling face forward fall and bites the ground with his face and rolls over onto his bad arm and starts to scream. This isn't a holler but a scream like a baby peeling or a dog getting cut, just his throat letting out sound.

Mary comes back with the bag of their supplies and their coats, and they put them on.

Marshall leans down and helps Roger to his feet and then ties his hands behind his back and they begin to walk back into the trees behind their house and into the ferns and fir trees.

"I deserve this," he says. "I wish I'd done this to my father. I really wish I had."

"Shut up," Mary says.

"I wish I'd done it to him. And then, I'd never have done anything to you."

"We don't want you to talk."

"Don't you want to understand why I did what I did?"

"No," Marshall says.

"I understand why you're doing what you're doing."

Marshall pushes him over, and he rolls down the hill and starts to sob.

"Get up," Martha says.

"No," he says.

"Get up," Martha says.

"I'm not getting up."

She kicks him in the arm. "Get up."

"No."

She kicks him in the arm again.

He gets up.

They walk for a long time through the dusky woods. It is very damp and water drips from the spider webs. And finally they come out of the woods and walk along a wire fence. Cattle graze at one of the edges of the field in the semi-darkness. They shift in the dark as they come closer. "Hi, cows," Martha says.

They pass the cows and cross the stream and then finally came to an old train bed. The rails were removed a long time ago. They walk on the old bed and finally come to one of the old coal shafts. The coal shaft went way down and into a mucky stream bed.

They stand in the rain and listen to the wind knock the branches together. Finally, Mary says, "What are you waiting for? Christmas isn't coming. Jump."

"Aren't you going to shoot me?"

"No."

"I'm not going to jump."

"Jump," Martha says.

"Jump," Mary says.

"Jump," Marshall says.

And he jumps. He falls into the hole. They listen to him fall and then they hear him splash deep in the earth in the muck.

He is gone. They listen to the wind knock the branches together and wait as it gets darker and darker, and then finally it is dark.

Roger doesn't yell.

Marshall shines the flashlight into the mineshaft to see whether they can see him. "He sank," Marshall says.

The girls look at each other and Marshall hopes to see some kind of emotion, but they are looking at each other almost as if they are copies of their porcelain dolls, just china and glass eyes.

They return to the house and clean the blood in the hallway and wash the rag with bleach. It is very late, and they can't go to sleep. Finally, near dusk, they all crawl into their beds.

Late in the morning their mother wakes them up.

"Where's Roger?"

"He's gone."

Aileen

Aileen sometimes spends the night at her church friend's church's house. Her friend is a thin widow who lives in a house in the middle of an overgrown farm across from the new golf course. Aileen packs her vinyl bag to change clothes and puts on her heavy gardening shoes. She says, "I'm going to go sit with Maggie."

Roger doesn't mind her leaving once the house is clean, but he asks her anyway, "Anything needs doing?" Aileen knows not to say *yes* to the question. He asks as if he himself would do it if it needs to be done. There is a division of labor. He earns paychecks. She does the work that doesn't earn cash, but still requires the expenditure of money on supplies. Aileen knows the correct answer. The correct answer is, *everything is done*. There is cold beer in the bottom of the cold box if he wants it.

Roger stands and picks up his paper and crosses to

her to look at her. She doesn't look at him as she shuffles away from him under the blue light coming down from the pasture. Rainwater specks the kitchen window glass. Roger stands next to her and she smells his aftershave, like rubbing alcohol and lemons. "Would you like a ride?" he asks.

She smiles. He never asks to give her a ride.

"I like to walk," she says.

"It's wet out," he says. "You'll get muddy."

"I've got my shoes," she says. "It's always wet out."

"It'd be no problem to give you a ride."

"I can walk. You have a nice night."

"You too," he says.

Aileen walks out into the dusk. It is oddly warm, not warm enough to not wear a mantle, but warm in the way that is not brisk. A drizzle falls but doesn't really get anything wet. It would be more trouble to carry an umbrella than to just put up with the few drops. Aileen hears and sees the school bus coming. She climbs down into the ditch like a fugitive. She climbs into the horsetails and muck and up into the thicket on the other side of the road and then into the canopy of fir trees. She stands on the golden bed of needles among the mushrooms and watches her kids climb down the bus steps, Martha and Mary. She isn't angry with them. She just doesn't feel connected to them anymore the way a mother should feel connected to her two daughters. They are her flesh. She doesn't want them to even know she exists. She loves them. She loves the idea of them more than she actually loves them. When they were babies she could never imagine that she would feel the way she feels now. She thought that was it for her life. She knows what she wants with the rest of her life, which is to be these girls' and her boy's mother. What else can she want to be? She can no longer be anything else. And then things happened and now she feels maybe she can no longer even be their mother. She is their mother because she has made them, but the idea of her being their mother is much different than the daily function of being their mother. She still feels she has been their mother when they were children who needed a mother. They curled against her while she knitted on the couch. They fell asleep as tiny children with dirt under their toenails, rips in their trousers from the barbwire fence, and their breath alkaline from water and milk. She told them not to climb on the wire fence. She told them to brush their teeth in the morning. Her job as a mother was to tell them. She felt when they were babies they would never become strangers to her. They would grow up to be hardly relatives to her at all even though she can glimpse long dead relations in them. They aren't strangers exactly, so much as strange to her. Orton and her combined to make a third, unrelated thing. She often imagined that her children would feel like an extension of herself. But that isn't the case at all. They are only the most distant extension of herself. She always told them, but they never told her anything except how she has not protected them from the things that she didn't know how to stop. She could not stop the rain from falling on them. She could not stop them from crying when the other school children were mean to them. There is so much that is beyond a mother's control.

When her daughters are well past she climbs out of the thicket and walks along to the side of the highway to her friend's house. Her friend lives in a tiny place on the edge of the garden in the blackberries. The place sits near the subdivision built near a golf course, itself built on land that once belonged to a farm.

Maggie's husband died many years ago. Maggie has no children. When Maggie told Aileen this, Aileen cupped her hands and said, "I'm so sorry." She was sorry. "So sorry that you don't have the blessing of children." Maggie just laughed. "What purpose would I have with children, Aileen? I only brought my mother grief."

"I never, really!" Aileen had never thought of women who wouldn't have children given the choice. That is their function: to populate the earth.

"The earth, Aileen, is populated enough."

"Why have children?"

"Not to populate the earth. Maybe because a person is vain and he wants to make more of himself."

Because they bring you joy, Aileen thought. Even though Maggie says this, it is so general and disconnected from her that Aileen doesn't take it as any statement about her own vanity. She had not chosen to have children. They just come from somewhere. They came from her feelings toward Orton. When they were little it was as close as she can imagine to the Divine Rapture. But that joy came with viciousness. Maybe any kind of intense experience is something for which a person finally has to pay? Pleasure is a debt.

Maggie asks again, "Why have children?"

Aileen hadn't asked for them, but when she realized she was pregnant, she felt very proud. She felt like she had done something. She realized she had a potential. She was the one who started this thing, and then she populated the dripping forest with more children. More of herself, not only copies of herself, but distant relations who thought things and felt things that she had no way of knowing about.

This was a conversation that she and Maggie had had a long time ago. They didn't need to discuss things like this now. Aileen arrived dripping from the fog. She stood on Maggie's porch. Maggie opens the door and asks, "Would you like some sherry?"

"I would, thank you," Aileen says. Maggie pours out

the bottle into the two glasses on the table. The room is lit with the light coming down across the empty field, from the stand of fir trees at the end of the subdivision. Specks of water coat the window; as they grow they move together and crawl into rivulets and run down the window. They sit for long stretches not talking and that is the thing about Maggie's house: silence.

With her daughters there is never silence, only nonsense. Darkness and silence are the two things they hate the most. Aileen came to Maggie's house to fill up on darkness and silence.

"It's getting late," Maggie says. She licks three papers and tilts the bottle of sherry towards Aileen.

"Yes."

She sits down and opens a drawer in the table and takes out the cards. They play whist for an hour.

"I thought I might sleep in the guest room tonight," Aileen says. "I desire a night's sleep for once. Please pardon my rudeness in inviting myself over. You did mention—"

"—yes. The offer is good. You can sleep here if that is what you would like."

"It is what I would like."

In the early morning she walks back to the house. When she comes inside she sees the kids have cleaned. They use too much bleach. It's still very early. Roger is gone. She lays down in her bed and sleeps. When she wakes sometime later, Roger is still gone. "Where is Roger?"

"Gone, Mom. He left on foot last night."

"Where too?"

"He got drunk and then left."

"Did he say where?"

"To the top of Saddle Mountain. "

"Did he say when he'd be back?"

"No. We are glad to see him go."

Mary

"Hi, girls," he says. It doesn't take a minute for them to see that their mother isn't home. The house is very clean, and she only leaves it that way when she is leaving it that way. When she is at home one of her chores would be in the middle of being worked on and everything else would be getting ready to be cleaned. The house, too, is quiet except for the dripping water from the eaves. Roger sits in the Chesterfield with a beer bottle and a little doily on the lamp stand. Even though it is dark enough the lamps in the house are off. They can see the backyard, blue and green drizzle and dust, through the kitchen windows. The furnace is on. The house smells like dust and the faint odor of gasoline. Roger stands to greet them. He still wears his work slacks and his short-sleeve drafting shirt decorated with an array of pencils and protractors in his breast pocket.

"Come on and give me a hug," he says.

"Please," Martha says. "Not in a million years."

He aims at Martha, but she starts up the stairs, taking with each step two stairs at a time, and leaves Mary behind her. Roger grabs Mary. The hardware in his pocket pinches her chest. She squirms away from him and he stands back and says, "Doesn't anyone love old dad anymore?"

"I have homework to do," Mary says. She turns to go to the stairs, but he grabs her on the soft flesh under her thigh. He tries to wiggle a finger up into her. He will leave a bruise. She feels the tip of his finger against her bone. The muscle of his hand grips the soft flesh there, too.

"You have some homework to do. All right."

Mary, without even thinking about it, extricates his hand. She squirms quickly up the stairs.

At the base of the stairs, Roger Carnation calls up after her. "Don't think I'm not coming up there for you two. Martha, it has been a long time."

Mary has a thick, damp feeling in her chest. She feels trapped on the stairs. She sits down on her bed. Martha sits at the desk chair and looks outside. "He is going to come up here."

"If he comes up for you, I will stab him," Martha says. Roger looks up to Mary in her room and she sits at her desk looking down at him.

"That isn't very smart of him," she says.

Upstairs, they listen to Roger and Marshall struggle. No sound came back from them. And then there is Marshall coming to the window. Roger begins to yell downstairs but they can't really tell what he is saying.

A steady splattering rain comes down. Mary sees Marshall on the front lawn. He has his trombone. He holds it in two parts. There is a new dent on the bell. Martha holds her finger to her head, pulls the trigger. Marshall sets his trombone down near the woodpile and then climbs up on the banister. He scrambles onto the roof. The gutter starts to peel away with a screech. There is damp, slippery moss on the roof. Mary pulls him into her window. They can hear Roger Carnation yelling downstairs. "Don't you come into the house that way. You can't come in the house without my permission. You are barred from this house. You come downstairs right now and go outside, or I'll come up there and strip the skin from your ass."

They hear him at the base of the stairs. He paces back and forth. At first they don't think he will come up the stairs. Mother has told him to stay downstairs. He is downstairs and now they can't go downstairs. Mother told him that she found one of Roger Carnation's socks in Martha's room. It is one of his special dress socks, silk, with a red band around it that Mother gave him for Christmas many years ago. Mary remembers when he opened the box with the socks. He took the socks out, and he smiled. He smiled and waved it to demonstrate that he was not happy with a sock for a present. But he didn't say anything. He said, "Thank you, dear." He just made his fake smile.

When she found the sock under Martha's bed that is when she made the rule of Roger never going upstairs, ever. "He can't come upstairs," Mary says.

"Because of the sock," Martha says, "Mother found out. You know what that sock was doing under my bed?"

"Don't say it," she says.

You already know," Martha says. "He wiped his cock with a sock." Mary looks at her and then leans into Martha. She starts to laugh and then Marshall starts to laugh. "You said," Mary says. "You said..."

"I know I said—"

"—you said cock. It rhymes with sock."

"I did."

They start to howl with laughter.

Roger stands at the base of the stairs and yells up to them, "You stop laughing."

He comes up the stairs. It sounds like he's too large to fit. The walls buckle as he squeezes himself through the narrow hallway. Cool air from the chilly living room pushes ahead of him. "What are you going to do?" Martha leans into the closet. She has the polished rifle that belongs to Roger Carnation. Mary is about to ask, "Where did you get that?" Martha hands the rifle to Marshall. Marshall doesn't look surprised. In fact, Marshall looks to Mary resigned, the way he does when he has to do the dishes. Even so, he says, "Now, what am I supposed to do with this?"

"You know," Martha says.

The three kids stand in Martha's room. The rain stops outside. Water rolls down the eaves of the house to the gutter. It makes a sloshing sound. Water splatters into the yard. The light becomes brighter now that the rain stopped. Martha's bed is made. Her shoes are lines under her bed. There is a nice pair of purple pumps. Martha never let Mary wear her shoes. Marshall inspects the rifle. "Are there bullets?"

"I almost forgot," Martha says. "Look to the boy to ask good questions like that."

She leans over and opens a pencil box on the desk. It is full of sparkling golden cases. There are bullets.

When she grabs a handful of them, one flips from her fingers onto the linoleum floor and rolls clattering to the chimney. Mary leans down to grab it. She doesn't understand why Roger took so long to get up the stairs and the last thing she wants is a bullet to come rolling down from upstairs.

Marshall slips the bullets into the rifle. The magazine makes an incredibly loud metal racket. Roger Carnation doesn't say anything about the noise. It made a loud click as each bullet entered the magazine.

And then he says, "I can hear you cretins."

But he still doesn't stick his head up.

"Martha, you come downstairs now with me, and I won't break Marshall's neck."

His voice now is right there on the stairs.

"Fuck you," Martha says.

Mary feels sick.

"Don't you use that kind of language with me. Your mother would agree with that." And he pulls himself into the hallway between the two bedrooms. The light shines on him so that he is just a shadow. Behind him they can see through Marshall and Mary's room. He faces the brick chimney next to the staircase. Marshall has the rifle and aims it toward him. Mary is unsure if he is actually going to fire the rifle. She looks and straight on through. Marshall doesn't really seem to even be in the room. His eyes are glassy. Mary wonders if he can actually hit anything with the rifle. It is so large and the hallway is so small. Roger turns. He sees that he sits right in the line of fire for the rifle. "What in the hell do you think you're doing?"

"I'm going to kill you."

He laughs. Roger starts moving towards the three of them.

"Marshall, what are you doing?" Martha asks.

"I don't know if I can do it," Marshall says.

Martha grabs the rifle then and Roger jumps towards them. It is slow going up the stairs. Martha pulls the trigger. The air fills with heat and light and smoke in the odor of something like crushed stone or dust. It goes through Mary's clothes. Roger yells. His shoulder is naked. She thinks she can even see pieces of his bone. Roger yells some more. But Mary still can't really hear, because of the loud noise of the shot that is so loud it feels like their eardrums have burst. Roger's arm is backwards. He falls down the stairs.

"I didn't kill him," Martha yells.

Martha pulls the rifle to one side like a crutch, and she falls down the stairs after him.

Mary and Marshall follow her out onto the porch. Roger limps across the lawn towards the forest. This time, Martha stands like a soldier or an archer. She stands like someone who has a lot of practice shooting rifles at people. She places the rifle against her shoulder and fires again. "Just hit him," and Roger stops in the middle of the thick grass between the house and the shed. It would almost be comical because on the crown of his head, Mary can see antlers affixed to the shed that look like they are coming out of Roger's skull. It is a good place to take a photograph, she realizes, if you want to make a joke like that.

Roger turns around, shuffling in the grass, and looks at them. "Martha, call the police," he says. "Your sister has gone completely mad."

Mary knows Martha isn't crazy. Mad can be two things.

"I should call someone," Marshall says.

"There's no one to call," Mary says. "We are in trouble if we do. They'll want to know why we shot him."

"It could have been an accident," Marshall says.

"I'm going to kill him," Martha says. "It's either going to be here at the house or where we planned."

"You can't kill me," Roger says.

"We are going to kill you," Marshall says.

"Do we have everything?" Martha asks.

"I'll go get it," Mary says. There is the bag they packed one day for the one day they killed Roger. That day is today. When they packed it Mary thought it was just a joke, for the game of "When we kill Roger." "What if," Martha said, "we actually kill him, what would we do?" And Mary said, "We need to have supplies so that we can quickly get the things we need because we won't be thinking clearly when it happens." And so in an old canvas bag, and not even sure where it has come from, perhaps it is one of Roger Carnation's Navy bags? They have filled it with a shovel, some old blankets, and a jug of water, bleach, and other supplies that Marshall says they need based on his reading of True Crime books. Everything becomes strange now. Mary realizes that Roger will die. It is just now a matter of actually following the steps they have discussed and those steps will mean that after they are done following them, Roger will be dead. She grabs her bag from the closet upstairs and returns. Roger lies flat on the ground and is screaming. Martha stands over him with the rifle pointed at the back of his head. Marshall helps him to his feet with his hands behind his back. They begin to walk into the trees behind the house and up into the trees.

"I knew this was coming," he says. "I wish I'd done this to people who had done me wrong. There is a list of them."

"Quiet," Martha says.

"I wish I had done it to my father, because then I'd never have done anything to you."

"We don't want you to talk."

"You need to understand why I did what I did."

"No," Mary says. "You may have your reasons and we might understand them but that doesn't mean we need to understand them. Knowing why you did them doesn't mean they had to happen."

"I understand," he says, "why you want to kill me."

Mary pushes him over. Roger totters and then falls like someone pushed over a garden rake. He rolls on the grass.

"Get up," Martha says.

"No," he says.

"Get up," Martha says.

"I'm not getting up," Roger says.

She kicks him in the arm. He howls. "Get up," she says.

"No."

She kicks him in the arm. He stands.

They walk through the damp forest. The first of the spring ground cover spreads under the trees in a faintly blue field. They come out of the forest to the cow field. Cattle graze at the edge of the field in the dusk. The cows move closer. Mary visits the cows on the way to school every morning.

They finally come to the old railroad bed. All of the hills around their house held coal a long time ago. When the mines closed the miners sealed the mine shafts. Erosion has opened a few.

They come to an open hole that you won't know is there unless you already know it is there. Martha must have already picked it out. Mary can hear water deep in the ground.

Marshall unties Roger's hands.

"Jump," Martha says. They all yell jump over and over again like it is a dare until Roger jumps. He falls into the hole. It is dark. In the forest Mary can't see anything. Just like that he is gone.

When they return to the house, they clean everything up. There isn't as much blood as Mary thought when things happened in the house. They take out the beer bottles. And Martha comes out to the porch with bottles and they all have one. It is the middle of the night. They each drink a beer sitting on the porch, and Mary is afraid for a second. "What if he comes back?" But the house seems so peaceful now. Finally, late at night, she crawls into bed and sleeps.

Martha

" Girls," he says. It's Roger Carnation. The first thing that Martha wants to do is to crush him. Somehow she imagines her hands inside the house and she would grab him between her thumb and index finger and with her giant hands snap him like a pea pod. It doesn't take a minute. Mother isn't home. There isn't the sound of the vacuum cleaner or washing machine. Martha thinks: My mother is home. She is the uncomfortable amount of labor she puts into keeping the house clean. Martha can't figure out why it takes so long to do this little amount except that she must not want to do it. Martha can't blame her; she wouldn't want to do it either. The house is quiet. She hears sparrows in the brambles across the lawn. She hears the sound of water on the house, it's as if the house floats on a lake, so much water comes from the sky and across the property. The backyard is blue and green in the drizzling dusk. The furnace ticks on, and the house smells like dust and a faint odor of paint thinner.

Roger sits in the Chesterfield with a bottle of beer. Roger stands to greet Mary and Martha. He still wears his work tie and his short sleeve shirt. He carries all kinds of crap in his pocket. He once showed Martha his slide rule; it was like two rulers strapped together with confusing lists of numbers in each margin. Martha thought it was a beautiful, arcane piece of machinery, but she would never tell Roger that. He shuffles in front of them attempting to compel them with the rulers and mechanical pencils in his pocket. "Come on, give me a hug," he says.

"Please leave us alone," Martha says. "I wouldn't give you a hug in a million years."

He aims at Martha, but she jumps around him and passes up the stairs, taking two steps at a time, and manages to get to the top of the stairs in a second and a half, less than two seconds at any rate. She bounces against a wall at the top of the stairs and runs into her room. Just look behind her, something is happening to Mary. She can hear them downstairs, and when Mary rushes up the stairs, her face is red. Her mouth is a dark hole with white teeth and sound comes out, sobbing.

"Don't think of my coming up there after you two. It has been a long time."

Martha doesn't pay attention to him anymore. He's downstairs. She looks over the side of the roof down to the back garden and sees Marshall. Marshal maneuvers on his bike, jumps off and lets it roll into the shed. Somehow he manages to keep his hands on his trombone case.

Roger is at the base of the stairs, making as if he is going to come up.

"He's going to come up here."

"If he comes up here, I'll kill him," Martha says.

"It wasn't very smart of him," Mary says.

Martha hears the rain on the roof. The wind rattles

the windowpanes. Downstairs there is the sound of the trombone. *Black stop wet stomp.*

Marshall rushes out to the front lawn. He holds his trombone. The bottom tubing has an agenda. He looks up to the window at Martha. She puts her pointer finger to her head and pulls the trigger. They talked about it a hundred times. Every time they talked about it they came to the same conclusion: Roger Carnation must die. Martha doesn't care how he will die. He just needs to be gone. But Mary and Marshal were interested in the plans and supplies. They drew plans. They made maps. They discussed what they'd do when they got the chance. Rogers is making it easy for them. He is drinking and he throws Marshall's trombone out into the front lawn. They can hear him shouting downstairs. Marshall climbs the sides of the house and comes up in through a window. Roger is downstairs yelling don't come back inside my house!

They hear him at the base of the stairs. Roger paces back and forth. At first she doesn't think he will come up the stairs. Aileen told him not to go upstairs anymore. She found the sock he'd used to wipe his cock that Martha had forgotten was there. She never looked under her bed, but she knew it was there and wondered if she could use it somehow to get Roger to leave her alone. It was one of his dress socks that Aileen had given him for Christmas the first year they moved into the house. Aileen had been looking to match the sock for a long time. The other sock was pinned to the wall in the laundry room. Aileen asked her daughter, "Were you wearing his socks?" "Why would I do that?" Aileen went downstairs. She told Roger never to go upstairs. The three of them are thinking the same thing. He is not allowed to come up the stairs. "You know what that sock was doing under my bed," Martha says.

Mary says, "I don't want to know."

"You already know," Martha says. "He wiped his cock with his sock."

Mary looks at her and then leans into her. She starts to laugh and then Marshall too starts to laugh. "You said," Mary says, "Cock."

"I know," Martha says. "Cock sock!"

"I did."

Roger stands at the base of the stairs. He yells at them to stop laughing.

It seems so silly then. They should just let Roger know they know what he's been doing. But that is against the rules. Martha doesn't know where the rules come from.

The rules aren't written. So he comes up the stairs. The rules may not be written but everyone knows them. What are we going to do? He's coming up the stairs. Martha picks up the hunting rifle that she's hidden in the closet. She gives the rifle to Marshall.

"What am I supposed to do with this?"

"You know."

The three of them stand in Martha's room. The rain has stopped outside, but everything still drips. The light from outside is much brighter as the rain has stopped. It is blue and fills the house with bluish light.

Marshall takes the rifle. "Where are the bullets?"

"I forgot," Martha says. She's glad that she showed him the rifle and that she didn't try to do something with the rifle herself. If she forgot the bullets, Roger would beat them all. "Leave it to the boy to ask questions like that."

Martha takes a handful of bullets from her pencil box. They are tiny like miniature lipsticks.

She drops one of the bullets on the linoleum floor and it rolls across towards the stairs. Mary grabs it.

Marshall slips a bullet into the rifle. And loads it and

fills the magazine. It makes a loud metallic click with each loaded bullet.

"I can hear you cretins," Roger says.

"Martha, you come downstairs now and have a beer with me, and I won't break Marshall's neck."

His voice is very loud. He is right there on the stairs.

"Fuck you," Martha says.

Mary's skin is white with a translucent coat of moisture. Martha can't figure it out.

"Don't you use that kind of language with me. Even your mother would agree with that." He jumps into the hallway between the two bedrooms. Outdoor light shines on him. He is just a silhouette. He's just a smudge. Marshall holds the rifle and lifts it. Roger turns and sees that he's in the sights of his own rifle. "What in the hell do you think you're doing?"

"I'm going to kill you," Marshall says.

"You can't do it," Roger says.

"Marshall, what are you doing?" Martha asks. Marshall has done nothing.

"I don't know if I can do it."

Roger jumps towards them. Martha grabs the rifle. She clicks the trigger, fills the small space with a huge explosion. She can't see if she hit him with a bullet. She doesn't know whether he's going to grab the rifle from her and then they will get it. It smells like the inside of a shoe or a gasoline tank. Martha can see again and she sees that something is wrong with Roger. His arm is attached backwards somehow. He tumbles down the stairs. She hasn't killed him. She hasn't killed him, yet. She drops down the stairs after him. She holds onto the rifle.

He isn't in the living room. He's on the porch. She follows him onto the porch. He is running to the shed where he keeps his own rifles. She stands steady on the porch, aims, and fires a bullet close enough to him that he can tell she can hit him. He stops on the grass.

"Marshall, your sister has gone crazy."

"Should I call someone?" Marshall asks.

"Don't call anyone," Martha says.

"We can still say it was an accident," Mary says.

"You can't kill me," Rogers says.

"You will be dead soon," Martha says.

"They will kill you if I don't," Marshall says.

"We have everything?" Martha asks.

"I'll get it," Mary says

Roger has suddenly changed. This is the change Martha has wanted to see in him all along. He looks sorry. He looks as if he didn't mean to do what he's done. He looks around. Rivulets of blood ran from the gash on his shoulder.

"Just take me to the hospital," he says. "I can tell them it was an accident. No one has to find themselves in trouble."

"Listen to him now," Martha says.

"Pretty much evens things out, doesn't it?" Roger asks.

"Not yet," Martha says.

Roger looks at them. He turns. He starts to run. Martha runs after him and almost slips on the grass. She catches up to him and trips him. He falls on his arm, rolling face forward in the muck and begins to scream. It is the sound of a baby peeling.

Mary comes back with their supplies and their coats. They put them on.

Marshall leans down and ties Roger's hands behind his back and leads him back into the trees behind the house into the ferns and fir trees.

"I deserve this," he says. "I wish that I killed my father. I really wish I had."

"Shut up," Martha says.

"I wish I'd done this to him. And then, I'd never have

done anything to you."

"We don't want you to talk."

"Don't you want to understand why I did what I did?"

"Now we don't," Marshall says.

"I understand why you're doing what you're doing."

Marshall pushes him over. Roger totters like a kicked vacuum cleaner. Roger rolls on the hill, starts to stop.

"Get up," Martha says.

"No," he says.

"Get up," Martha says.

"I'm not getting up so that you can kill me."

She kicks him in the arm. "Get up!"

"No."

She kicks him in the arm again.

He gets up.

They walk for a long time to the dank woods. It is very damp. Water drips from the boughs. They come out of the woods and walk along a fence. Massive white cows, their hooves plopping into the mud and pulling free with pops, cross the field looking for grass handouts. Mary always feeds them. Their lips are white, and their tongues are almost black in the darkness. "Hi, cows," Mary says.

They walk past the cows, across streams, finally come to an old train grade. The railroad tracks and ties were removed a long time ago. They're tiny saplings coming up in the road. They walk along the old bed and finally come out to one of the old coal mine shafts. The coal shafts go way down into the earth. The sound of water whispers down in there somewhere.

They stand in the rain. Finally, Martha says, "What are you waiting for? Jump!"

"Aren't you going to shoot me?"

"No."

"I'm not going to jump."

Marshall unties his hands.

"Jump," Martha says.

"Jump," Mary says.

"Jump," Marshall says.

Roger jumps into the hole and they listen to him fall. They can hear him splash deep in the mud below the ground.

They listen to the wind pop the branches together. It gets darker and darker, then finally it is dark.

He didn't yell.

"He's dead now," Marshall says.

They return to the house and clean up the blood in the hallway. They wash the walls with bleach. They scour the house, looking for everything. Martha laughs. She grabs bottles of beer to drink on the porch. Mary and Marshall sip their own bottle. They all stare out into the darkness. Everything feels okay. Finally, Martha says it is time to sleep. Because she knows that she will be able to sleep the entire night and when she wakes up in the morning everything bad will have happened yesterday.

Carnation

Aileen tells Roger, "I'm going to go sit with Maggie."
Maggie is her friend from church, and she lives in
the old farmhouse on the farm that no longer grows
anything across from the golf course. Just a matter of
time before it becomes a new subdivision. When she first
says this Roger doesn't know what she means. He thinks
she's going to go there for a visit. She will be back before
everyone turns in. She rushes around the house making
last-minute adjustments. She returns from the bedroom
with her vinyl bag she's only used before when she had
to go overnight to the hospital when they found a lump.
The lump turned out to be nothing. It was everything
before the doctor, a short man with a tower of bright red
hair, said it was nothing to worry about. Better to be safe
than sorry. You did the right thing. Now you can rest
easy. Aileen has a change of clothes and her heavy garden
shoes. She'll be gone for the night. Roger doesn't mind

her leaving the house. He wishes she'd do it more often. He tried to talk her into returning to her mother's house in Kentucky, but she said she couldn't leave him alone, by himself. He prefers her daughters to her now. It wasn't always that way. He can hardly remember when it wasn't that way—but it wasn't always that way—or they would never sleep in the same room. They slept in separate beds just as his parents had slept in separate beds. She once tried to get a queen-sized bed. "That is all fine and good," he said. "But I need to sleep sometime." The house is clean since she is leaving. He asks her anyway: "Do you have anything you need to do?" He asks this question not meaning he will do anything if she hasn't done it. He asks the question so he can make a face at her if she hasn't done it. The correct answer is, "Everything is done." She says, "Everything is done." She adds, "There's cold beer in the bottom of the ice box if you want it."

Roger stands up and folds his paper. He stands to look at her. She won't look at him. She shuffles into the blue light. She retreats into the kitchen.

"It's wet out," he says. "You'll get muddy."

"I've got my shoes on," she says. "It might let up."

"It'd be no problem to give you a ride."

"I can walk. It's always wet. That's why I have my shoes. You have a nice night, Roger," she says.

"You too," he says. He returns the cup of coffee to the sideboard. When she opens the door, he hears the wind rubbing the branches. Falling water from the gutter splatters on the lawn. The rain barrel can't contain the flow. It is always full. He empties it because mosquitoes fill the water, tiny larva with feather-like wings spiral in the dark. He doesn't want a mosquito farm right under his window. The floorboards in the kitchen creak. Aileen wanted the sound fixed. She said she thought she would go through the floor one of these days. Roger said if you do, that'll serve you right, you fat bitch. He tapped the floor with his foot. It is solid but the give is more than he planned on.

He's through with his third beer when Martha and Mary come home from school. "Hi, girls," he says. "Come on, give me a hug," he says.

"Please..." Martha says. Always lip on that one. She's the only one who listens to him anyway. She is the one who talks back, but she is a good girl. It's Mary who never says anything that is the trouble. Mary always watches him. She is careful with what she says. "Not in a million years," Martha says.

Martha, she starts up the stairs, taking each of the steps as quickly as she can. That leaves Mary behind her. He shuffles toward her trying to hug her. She squirms away. She shuffles backward up a stair. She stares at him like she might look into the face of a corpse. "Doesn't anyone love old dad anymore?"

"I have homework to do," Mary says. She turns to go up the stairs. Roger grabs a handful of her flesh under her thigh and half lifts her from the stairs. He manages to wiggle a finger under her skirt and into her underpants. He feels sick to his stomach. He wants to hold her and rip her into pieces at the same time. The tip of his middle finger brushes her pubic hair and then enters a soft and warm cavity. "You have some homework to do all right," he says.

Mary twists his hand, nearly breaking his fingers. She squirms rapidly up the stairs where he is not allowed.

Still at the base of the stairs, Roger Carnation yells up after her. "Don't think of my coming up there for you two! It has been a long time." The words are coming out more rapidly than his thoughts.

As he watches Mary's white socks and black shoes disappear up the stairs, he feels himself stiffen. If a man's dick goes away on its own accord, that's the worst thing. He thinks for a while before he met Aileen and her daughters that perhaps erections were a kind of demonic possession. His body was one way and then something happened to him and it was another way. He could only think about one thing. He would rather think about other things. To even say this was thought wasn't correct. What was the difference between demons and daemons beside the extra "a?" He can't very well go up after them because then what he wanted would be public. Anyone could surmise the situation, Roger figured, a man and a house full of women. What he was doing was not allowed, technically, but he wasn't related to these two girls. He wasn't their real father. In the Bible, they would belong to him. Their real father was no kind of father anyway. Marshall would be home soon anyway.

Aileen brewed the beer herself from an old family recipe. She collected the bottles during the summer on walks to town while Roger was at work. She boiled them and then after brewing the beer she filled the bottles and capped each one. She made root beer at the same time. Roger didn't drink much. He never looked for the bottles. But when Aileen brought them out, he would drink them. He drank while in the Navy but everyone drank. It was the way a person conducted himself when on shore leave. Right now though he isn't drunk but he has a fine steady hum in his head and he would like to keep that going, because the heat from the furnace feels nice. The house only has natural light downstairs. But incandescent light falls from upstairs. It's shining down the driveway and onto his car parked in its place.

Drinking in the Navy was a pastime and an art. He remembers a three-day bender. Well, he remembers part of the bender and the aftermath. It gained a kind of collateral with the other sailors. He never had anything like this happen to him. He went upstairs with a Korean whore. She wore a green plaid skirt and a white shirt with a blue ribbon around her neck. She took him up to a room with an unmade bed that smelled like mold and incense. She offered him something to smoke and he smoked it. It tasted like smoking damp earth. He had a very happy, funny feeling body after smoking it and spent the time in bed with her and then woke on his back in the street with his shoes on but no socks. Someone had stolen his socks. His wallet of course was gone. Luckily he still had his dog tags. When he returned to the ship, he checked in. There was medication for someone after an experience like that.

He prefers this situation to that. No memory of what it was like. As if it was a recovered experience from another life, like reincarnation. He takes a sip of Aileen's beer. It is bitter and sharp, and leaves a happy feeling in his body. He thinks maybe this is enough for tonight. Mary's thigh was heavy as she wiggled to escape the stairs. These girls really know what they are doing. They drive a man crazy.

He walks to the base of the stairs. "Can one of you girls come down?"

No answer.

"Girls?" No answer. It would be the least they could do since he puts the food in the fridge and the roof over their heads.

He sits in his chair.

The gravel snaps under Marshall's bike. He glances out the window and there he is riding his bike, balancing his asinine tuba or whatever it is that he plays. Marshall dismounts and drops the case on the porch. The house shakes. Now Aileen is sure to fall through the floor. It's a trombone, not a tuba. Marshall takes his bike to the shed. Roger stamps his feet on the porch. It is cold outside. He forgot it is cold. He takes the case and can't figure out how to open it. It doesn't just open. There must be a latch. When he finds the latch he can't get it to work.

"What are you doing, Roger?"

Roger looks up. Marshall always expects something from Roger and Roger can't figure out what it is. He despises Marshall for it at first because Roger doesn't know how to do whatever it is that Marshall wants him to do. Roger thinks of him as the booby prize that came along with Aileen and her two tender daughters. He didn't think of the children at the time. They seemed unimportant to him. He was interested in Aileen because after they went to the movies, they could park under the Wagoner Bridge like teenagers. They even had sex, unlike teenagers, sure of themselves and what they were doing in the car. She knew what she wanted from him, and it seemed such a small thing to her. He would trade. And then she dumped him.

She said, "I was mistaken about you Roger. I made a big mistake. I've put myself at your mercy. I'm a divorced woman with children. You can do better than me."

The phrase, "at your mercy," was something he could hear more of. No one had ever been at his mercy before.

To think this woman was at his mercy seems odd and strange. She wore bright lipstick and a floral dress and a black scarf. It was just her and him. He paid for dinner, dropped her off at the rooming house where she lived with the kids. Although he hardly saw the children, he sometimes took them all to church on Sunday. There were two girls, one in middle school, pretty and seemingly prim, and the other in high school. Martha even then with lips with hastily broken off lipstick, seemed to know more about things than a girl like her should. She asked him, "What are you looking at?"

In fantasies, Roger of course thought about the girls but that was hardly a real thing. The real thing was he looked forward to going to church on Sunday to see the girls in their dresses and afterwards to buy everyone lunch and have Martha sit next to him, very close to him, and ask when her Mom and he were going to move in together.

"We would have to be married," Aileen said.

When Aileen cut him off, of course, he knew she was really forcing his hand. And so he told her he couldn't live without her and her family. Within the month, he gave her the ring.

She started to cry and said, "Oh Roger oh yes." Before they had gone to the Wagoner Bridge she said, "I want to let your family know now."

"Now?" he asked.

They went to the gas station payphone. He realized he hadn't even told them he was seeing Aileen. He wanted to go to the bridge and he could tell his mother and then he could tell her he was going to be married. "We have to go now," she said. After Aileen talked to his mother, he talked to his mother. "I don't believe it. I don't even know this woman," his mother said.

"I'm going to get married, mother," he said.

His mother started crying and when he hung up the phone he looked at Aileen and she lay her head on his shoulder. "I'm so happy," she said.

You're so relieved is more like it, Roger thought.

Roger opens the case and lifts out the trombone. He removes the mouthpiece from the tiny red velvet-lined case in one corner. In school Roger played the trumpet but he hated trumpet players. Even worse he hated practicing and without practice playing songs was never enjoyable. Instead it was a painful exercise in not knowing the notes and faking it. He inserts the mouthpiece into the trombone.

"Roger, I don't think that's a good idea."

"I'm going to play this thing," he says.

Marshall leaves him on the porch. Roger has the

trombone and makes a thick rumble bass note. He begins to make the noise over and over again.

Roger comes into the house and tosses the trombone with a jangle by the front door. When he walks into the kitchen he doesn't even look at Marshall but pulls open the fridge and takes out a beer bottle. Marshall is boiling hot dogs.

"Hotdogs. That's carnival food, son. It'll give you cancer and who knows what else. We've got real food in the freezer. Venison. Trout. Liver."

"I'm not that hungry. I just want to eat and study."

"Shit, no wonder you have such shit for grades."

The hot dogs finish boiling. Marshall takes them from the pot. He heads for the stairs with his plate.

"Where you going in such a hurry?"

"Marshall, honey," Roger hollers at the base of the stairs. "You left your horn by the front door."

"I'll pick it up later."

"It's going out in the yard," Roger yells. He picks it up.

"I warned you!" Marshal can hear the front door open. He rushes downstairs and Roger has the trombone in his hands and throws it out the open door. The trombone sails downstairs. The rim of the horn knocks on the banister and the trombone flips up and drops right into the daffodil bed with a sharp clang. Marshall rushes down the steps and Roger closes and locks the door behind him.

Roger turns to drink from the bottle and sit down and wait for Roger to knock. He hears a metal noise from outside. The gutter separates from the house with a sharp shriek.

Roger yells, "Do not come in the house that way! You can't come into the house without my permission. You are barred from this house. You come downstairs right now and get outside, or I'll come up there and strip the skin from your ass."

Roger paces at the bottom of the stairs. He drinks from his bottle. He thinks of himself as a dog on a leash. This is his damn house. He can go up the stairs if he so chooses. Every thread of clothes on those kids' backs came out of his pay. They start to laugh. It's no kind of soft laughter, but deep from the belly, out of the throat laughter. They are laughing at him. He can hear it coming from the windows outside and down the stairs.

Roger looks upstairs to see if he can see them. He can't.

He goes up the stairs. He isn't even thinking now. The entire house creeks and shakes. "I can hear you cretins!" Roger says. But he waits right at the top of the stairs. Martha comes downstairs now. "Have a beer with me and I won't break Marshall's neck."

"Fuck you," Martha says.

"Don't you use that kind of language with me. Your mother would agree with that." He can't believe the insolence, the cheek of these children. He pulls himself up into the hallway between two bedrooms. He hasn't been up here for over a year. The light from the windows and the lamps makes him blind. He can feel the rough brickwork of the chimney with his hands as he waits for his eyes to adjust. He realizes that someone is pointing his rifle at him.

He is a sitting duck.

"What in the hell do you think you're doing?"

"I'm going to kill you."

"You can't do it."

Roger moves towards the three of them. This has become a serious problem. He is a bit addled from the beer and playing the trombone. The slide threw him off. He could play the trumpet; he really could make a sound with a trumpet. He is fuzzy from yelling. This has to stop.

"Marshall, what are you doing?" Martha says.

"I don't know if I can do it."

She grabs the rifle from Marshall. Roger sees his chance. He jumps towards them but he is trying to jump up stairs. Before he can get far, Marshall actually pulls the trigger. It is loaded. He didn't think it was loaded. For an instant Roger doesn't know anything. Complete blackness. There isn't even pain. Then he's aware that he isn't dead. They are still upstairs. Something is incredibly wrong. He still doesn't feel any pain. Then he can't move the left side of his body. A smell like a rusty can. He's falling. He tumbles down the steps and when he hits the bottom of the stairs with his good arm he pushes himself up against the wall and runs to the door. He can't open it with his good hand. He opens it with his bad hand. The knob is cold. First he thinks that he can hide in his shed. He can lock the door behind him. And then he realizes his other rifles are there. He can grab a rifle and then he can fight back. How to use a rifle with one hand? These kids don't know what they have gotten themselves into. He's been in a war. He's seen combat. He knows how to deal with something like this.

Something snaps past his ear. He stops and turns. Martha stands on the porch, her arms cocked under the rifle stock; her legs spread apart in a triangle. She has the rifle loaded and pointed at him. Behind her, looking extremely scared, are Marshall and Mary. "Marshall," Roger says, "Call the police. Your sister is nuts."

"Should I call someone?" Marshall asks her. If she is crazy, why in the hell would he ask her anything?

"There's no one to call," Martha says. "We are in trouble if we do. They will want to know why we shot him."

"It could be an accident," Marshall says.

"I'm going to kill him," Martha says. "We are going to do what we planned." When she says this, "as we planned", he realizes this isn't an accident, that this isn't a bit of revenge out of hand; they're prepared. In fact, they were waiting just like he was waiting for Aileen to leave the house.

"You can't kill me," Roger says.

"You are going to die. She will kill you if I don't," Marshall says. Roger almost wants to laugh at that boy. He has done nothing. Martha is the one he should be afraid of.

"Do we have everything?" Martha asks.

"I'll get it," Mary says. Roger realizes that they're going to kill him. Martha will see him dead. There is nothing he can do about it. What to do? If he moves she will shoot again. And maybe she won't kill him with that first bullet but there are ten more bullets. He can't survive ten shots. She doesn't have any kind of aim. "Just take me to the hospital. I can tell them it was an accident. No one has to get in any trouble."

"Listen to him now," Martha says.

He sympathizes with what she is doing. It is something that he himself would have done if given the chance. His old man should have had a bullet put into his skull. "This pretty much even things out, doesn't it?" He asks.

"It doesn't even begin to even things out," Martha says. "I should stick this rifle up your ass and give you a lead enema."

Roger doesn't believe that she is this angry. She feels she is supposed to be this angry. She was the one who started it. But as a matter of killing him she will absolve herself of this filth that she has created. She has perpetrated this in the house. He is just a man and vulnerable to temptations. He turns to run. Better to risk a shot than the sure thing of a rifle to his head. They won't kill him. He will escape. If he escapes he might be able to survive if he makes it to the trees. The rifle doesn't fire. He thinks he's made it. But then his legs are kicked out from underneath him. He hits the ground. A white explosion of pain on his arm stops him from moving. He looks at the sky. Oh, he is screaming again. His throat hurts and the sound coming out of it hurts his ears. It hurts coming out and coming in.

Marshall pulls him onto his feet. Roger stands wobbly, looking around at the three of them. Mary has a bag full of supplies. They really had this planned. There's no way now he can survive.

"I deserve this," he says. "I would have done this to my father. I really wish I had."

"Shut up," Martha says.

"I wish I had done it to him. And I've never done anything to you."

"We don't want you to talk."

"You should think about what you are doing—" Roger says.

Marshall pushes him over and he rolls down the slope until he hits his arm again. He almost passes out. He doesn't want to get up.

"I'm not getting up."

Martha kicks him in the arm. Pass out, he thinks.

There is a blue electrical pain that sears through his entire body. He struggles to stand. He holds his body with his legs in a squat. Sweat drips from his eyebrows.

They walk for a long time. It is dusk. It is very damp. His mouth catches spider webs. He can't reach out to pull them down.

They walk along a flat rail bed thick with alder and cedar saplings. Finally, they come to a hole in the ground. Roger realizes it is one of the coal shafts that riddle the forest. Most of them have been sealed. A stream has opened this one up. There is the sound of water down in the depths.

"Jump!" they tell him.

Marshall removes something from his hands.

"Jump," they are saying. He is no longer certain which one of them is saying this. Aren't they going to shoot? Now. They all say it over and over again. Jump! So he hops. For an instant he is free of the pain in his arm. His knees pop from the sockets. A cool weight presses against his hips. Light flickers on the walls around him and then it is dark. He feels the mud slide around his waist and it eases up to his shoulder pits. He can't move his legs. He can't move his arms. He wants to squirm or paddle but the mud draws around his arms. The surface of the water licks at his neck. The world is bright and dim, cool and warm.

www.ingramcontent.com/pod-product-compliance
Lightning Source LLC
Chambersburg PA
CBHW050423260626
47156CB00003B/1127